OLD TALES
RETOLD

D1648029

Lu Hsun

Pencil drawing by
Tao Yuan-ching

OLD TALES RETOLD

Lu Hsun

FOREIGN LANGUAGES PRESS
PEKING 1972

First Edition 1961
Second Edition 1972

Translated by
Yang Hsien-yi and Gladys Yang

Printed in the People's Republic of China

CONTENTS

THE AUTHOR'S PREFACE 1

MENDING HEAVEN 5

THE FLIGHT TO THE MOON 16

CURBING THE FLOOD 30

GATHERING VETCH 51

FORGING THE SWORDS 74

LEAVING THE PASS 96

OPPOSING AGGRESSION 109

RESURRECTING THE DEAD 124

The Author's Preface

This is a small volume of stories, yet the interval between the time when I started it and its completion was quite long: a whole thirteen years.

The first tale, "Mending Heaven," originally entitled "The Broken Mount," was written in the winter of 1922. My idea at that time was to take material for some stories both from antiquity and the present age. "The Broken Mount" was a first attempt, based on the legend of Nu-wa who melted stones to mend the vault of heaven. I started off in sober earnest, though simply using Freudian theories[1] to explain the origin of creation — the creation of men as well as of literature. I forget what made me put down my pen half way to read the newspaper, where as ill luck would have it I found an article by a critic whose name I have forgotten on *Breeze over the Orchids*[2] by Wang Ching-chih. With tears in his eyes, the critic besought young writers to produce no more such effusions. This miserable plot struck me as so ludicrous that when

---

[1] Lu Hsun was at one point interested in the Freudian theory of psycho-analysis, but he was never influenced by it; in fact he adopted a sceptical attitude. In an article he wrote in 1933 called "Listening to a Talk on Dreams," he pointed out the fallacies of this theory.

[2] *Breeze over the Orchids* was an anthology of verse. The critic was Hu Meng-hua, a student of the Southeast University.

I returned to my story, try as I might, I could not prevent a little man in antique dress from appearing between the legs of the goddess. That was how I lapsed from seriousness to facetiousness. Facetiousness is the worst enemy of writing; I was most displeased with myself.

So I decided to write no more tales of this sort and, when publishing *Call to Arms,* I appended it as the first and last attempt of its kind.

That was when our noted critic Cheng Fang-wu[1] was brandishing his axe at the gate of the Creation Society under the flag of "Adventures of the Soul." On the charge of "vulgarity," with some swings of his axe, he annihilated *Call to Arms*, and only described "The Broken Mount" as a fine piece of writing — though not without faults. Frankly speaking, far from convincing me, this made me despise this warrior. I have no contempt for vulgarity: I delight in being vulgar. As for historical

---

[1] Cheng Fang-wu, from Hsinhua, Hunan, was one of the chief members of the Creation Society at the time of the "May the Fourth" Modern Literary Movement. He was a well-known literary critic in that period, advocated romanticism and considered literature as the self-expression of the writer. After the May the Thirtieth Movement of 1925 he began to sympathize with the revolution, and his literary views also began to change. Between 1927 and 1928 he and Kuo Mo-jo started a revolutionary literary movement, but soon he gave up literary activities and turned to do revolutionary educational work. After Lu Hsun published his first collection of short stories *Call to Arms*, Cheng wrote a review of it for the *Creation Quarterly*, Vol. II, No. 2 (January 1924). Starting from his viewpoint that literature was the self-expression of the writer, he erroneously concluded that such stories by Lu Hsun as *Madman's Diary, Kung I-chi, Medicine, Tomorrow* and *The True Story of Ah Q,* were "naturalistic," superficial and vulgar. However, he maintained that "Mending Heaven," "though containing passages not good enough," was nevertheless a "masterpiece" showing that the author would "enter the palace of pure literature." The "adventures of the soul" mentioned here is a quotation from Anatole France: "La critique litteraire est une aventure de l'ame parmi les chefs-d'œuvre." This was quoted by Cheng Fang-wu in his review.

stories, to my mind those based on extensive research with sound evidence for every word are extremely hard to write, even though they are sneered at as "novels smacking of the school-room"; whereas not much skill is needed to take a subject and write it up freely, adding some colouring of your own.

Besides, "The fish can tell whether the water is hot or cold."[1] In vulgar parlance, "A man knows his own illness." The second half of "The Broken Mount" is far too sloppily put together to be called a fine piece of writing. If I allowed readers to believe the judgement of that adventurer, they would be deceived and I would be deceiving them. So I cut this story out of the second edition of *Call to Arms* to strike back at this "soul" — that volume was wholly occupied by rampant "vulgarities."

In the autumn of 1926, I was living alone in a stone house in Amoy, looking out over the ocean. I leafed through old books, no breath of life around me, a void in my heart. But letters kept coming from the Weiming Press in Peking asking for articles for our magazine. Since I was in no mood to think of the present, old memories stirred in my heart, and I wrote the ten essays in *Dawn Blossoms Plucked at Dusk*. And, as before, I picked up ancient legends and the like in preparation for writing the eight stories in *Old Tales Retold*. But no sooner had I finished "The Flight to the Moon" and "Forging the Swords," published under the title "Mei Chien Chih," than I had to hurry to Canton, once more setting the project aside. Later on, though I found fresh scraps of material and wrote some hasty sketches, I never managed to put the whole in order.

Now at last I have made up some sort of volume. Most of it is still in the form of hasty sketches, not worthy

[1] A Buddhist phrase dating from the Sung Dynasty.

of the name of "story" according to the manuals of literature. In some places the narrative is based on passages
in old books, elsewhere I gave free rein to my imagina-
tion. And having less respect for the ancients than for
my contemporaries, I have not always been able to avoid
facetiousness. Thirteen years have passed, still I have
made no progress: this does seem to be "trashy stuff like
'The Broken Mount.'" At least I have not made the
ancients out as even more dead than they are, and this
may justify the book's existence for a while.

December 26, 1935

Mending Heaven

I

Nu-wa[1] woke with a start.

She was frightened out of a dream, yet unable to
remember what she had dreamed; conscious only, rather
crossly, of something missing as well as of a surfeit of some
kind. Ardently, the quickening breeze wafted her energy
over the universe.

She rubbed her eyes.

This way and that through the pink sky floated wisps
of rock-green clouds, behind which winked stars. In the
blood-red clouds at the horizon was the glorious sun, like
some fluid orb of gold lapped in a waste of ancient lava;
opposite, the frigid white moon seemed as if made of
iron. But she did not notice which was setting or which
rising.

The whole earth was a tender green. Even the pines
and cedars, whose leaves fall so seldom, were strikingly
fresh. Great blossoms, peach-pink or bluish-white, clearly
visible near by, faded in the distance into a motley mist.

"I've never been so bored!"

---

[1] A mythical empress or goddess of ancient times. According to
Chinese mythology the first men were made out of mud by Nu-wa.

With this reflection she sprang to her feet, stretched her perfectly rounded arms so compact of strength and yawned at the sky. At once the sky changed colour, turning a miraculous flesh-pink so that for a moment Nu-wa was lost to sight.

She walked through this flesh-pink universe to the sea, and the lines of her body merged with the luminous, rose-tinted ocean, only a zone of pure white remaining visible at her waist. The astounded waves rose and fell in perfect order spattering Nu-wa with foam. The reflection of this pure white flesh flickered in the water as if it meant to scatter in all directions. But without observing it, not knowing what she did, she went down on one knee and scooped up a handful of soft mud. She kneaded this several times till she had in her hands a small creature much like herself.

"Ah! Ah!"

Though she had made it herself, she couldn't help wondering if it hadn't been in the mud all the time like a segment of potato. She started with surprise.

This was happy surprise, however. She went on with a verve and zest hitherto unknown, breathing into the figures, mingling her sweat with them.

"Nga! Nga!" The little creatures were calling out.

"Ah! Ah!" She felt with a pang that something was streaming out from every pore of her body. The ground was misted over with white, milky vapour. She mastered her panic and the little creatures stopped crying.

Some of them said to her: "Akon! Agon!"

"Ah, you darlings!" Without taking her eyes off them, Nu-wa tapped their plump white cheeks with her muddy fingers.

"Uvu! Ahaha!" They were laughing. For the first time in the universe she heard laughter. For the first time she laughed herself, unable to stop.

6

Caressing them, she went on with her task. The finished figures circled round her, going further off by degrees, talking more volubly. By degrees, too, she ceased to understand them. Her ears were simply filled with a medley of cries till her head began to swim.

Into her long drawn out joy had crept weariness. Her breath was nearly exhausted, her sweat nearly spent. Moreover her head was swimming, her eyes were dim, her cheeks burning. Gone was all her excitement; she was losing patience. Yet she toiled on, hardly knowing what she did.

At last the pain in her back and legs forced her to stand. Leaning against a smooth, high mountain, she raised her head to look round. The sky was full of white clouds like the scales of a fish, while below was a deep, dark green. For no apparent reason the sight displeased her. Moodily she put out one hand to pluck a wistaria which reached from the mountain to the sky. On it were clusters of huge purple flowers. She threw it down on the ground and the earth was covered with petals, half purple, half white.

She flicked it and the wistaria rolled over in the muddy water, sending up a spray of mud which falling on the ground turned into little creatures like those she had made. But most of these looked stupid and repulsive, with heads like deer, eyes like rats. Too preoccupied to pay any attention, eagerly and impatiently, as if in sport, she flicked the muddy wistaria faster and faster, till it twitched on the ground like a coral snake scalded by boiling water. Drops of mud splashed off the vine and while still in mid-air changed into small howling creatures, which crawled off in every direction.

Barely conscious, she swung the wistaria yet more wildly. Not only were her back and legs aching, but even her arms were tired. She had to crouch down to rest her head on a mountain. Her jet black hair streamed

7

over the mountain top. After regaining her breath, she closed her eyes with a sigh. The wistaria fell from her fingers to lie limp and exhausted on the ground.

II

Crash!!!

As heaven split asunder and the earth burst open, Nu-wa awoke with a start to find herself sliding towards the southeast. She put out a foot to stop herself, only to discover nothing there. Throwing one arm around a mountain peak, she managed to break her fall.

Water, sand and rocks were raining down on her head from behind. When she looked over her shoulder, water poured into her mouth and both her ears. She hastily lowered her head — the earth was heaving and shaking. Luckily this soon subsided, and stepping back she sat down on solid ground to wipe the water from her forehead and eyes and see what exactly had happened.

The scene was one of utter confusion. All over the earth great torrents were cascading. Here and there, in what she took to be the ocean, leaped and towered sharp-crested billows. She waited, dumbfounded.

At last great calm was restored. The largest waves were no higher than the old peaks, and where the land must be projected jagged ridges of rock. Turning to the sea, she saw several mountains sweeping towards her, whirling round in the tumbling waves. Afraid they might bump her foot, she put out a hand to stop them. That was when she noticed, in the gullies, some creatures she had never set eyes on before.

She drew one of the mountains to her for a closer look. Vomited on the ground beside these creatures was something resembling gold dust and powdered jade mixed with chewed pine needles and meat. Slowly, one by one, they raised their heads, and Nu-wa's eyes widened when she recognized the little creatures she had made. They had covered their bodies in the most curious fashion, and some of them had snow-white beards growing from the lower part of their faces — beards matted by the brine like pointed poplar leaves.

"Ah, ah!" She gave a cry of fright and astonishment. Her flesh crept as if a caterpillar had crawled over it.

"Save us, Goddess. . . ." One with a white beard on his chin had raised his head. Between retchings he said in a broken voice: "Save us. . . . Your humble subjects . . . are in quest of immortality. None of us foresaw this disaster, the collapse of heaven and earth. . . . Mercifully we have met you, Goddess. . . . Save our worthless lives. . . . And give us an elixir . . . to make us immortal." He raised and lowered his head in the strangest manner.

"What's that?" asked Nu-wa, quite baffled.

Several of them started speaking at once, retching as they invoked the Goddess, all going through the same strange motions. This was so exasperating that she bitterly repented the action which had brought such bewildering trouble upon her. She looked helplessly around. A school of giant tortoises[1] was sporting in the ocean. Surprised and pleased, she lost no time in putting the mountains on their backs and giving the order: "Take them to some quieter place!"

The giant tortoises nodded and trooped off into the distance. She had pulled the mountains too hard, however, so that one of the creatures with a white beard on his chin had fallen off. . . . He could not even swim,

---

[1] These giant tortoises of the ocean were considered divine in ancient mythology.

9

let alone overtake the others, but prostrated himself on the beach, slapping his face. Nu-wa pitied him but paid no attention to him — she simply had no time to attend to such matters.

She sighed, her heart grew lighter. She turned around and saw the water lapping round her subside considerably, revealing broad stretches of earth and rock with a multitude of small creatures in the clefts of the rock, some stiff and stark, others still moving. One of these, in fact, was staring stupidly at her. He was covered with strips of metal, while despair and fear contended on his face.

"What happened?" she asked casually.

"Alas! Heaven visited calamity upon us!" he answered piteously. "Chuan Hsu, in defiance of right, attacked our king. Our king decided to fight him in accord with Heaven's will and we battled in the country. But Heaven did not protect the just — our army was thrown back. . . ."[1]

"What's that?" Nu-wa, never having heard talk of this kind before, was utterly amazed.

"Our army was thrown back. Our king knocked his head against the Broken Mount, smashed the pillar of heaven and the support of the earth and perished himself. Alas! This is truly. . . ."

"That's quite enough! I can't understand a word." Turning her head away she discovered a proud and joyful face — its owner was also covered with strips of metal.

"What happened?" Now that it dawned on her that these little creatures could vary so much in expression, she hoped to elicit a different, comprehensible answer.

---

[1] This refers to the mythical fight between Chuan Hsu, a descendant of the Yellow Emperor, and the giant Kung Kung, also known as Kang Hui. The giant in his rage at being defeated knocked his head against the mountain which propped up the vault of heaven. Then heaven cracked open and the earth sagged southeastwards.

"The human heart harbours evil. Kang Hui with the heart of a swine actually aspired to the imperial throne. Our king fought him in accord with the will of Heaven. We battled in the open country, and Heaven did indeed protect the just. Our army was victorious and Kang Hui was slain on the Broken Mount."

"What's that?" She was still at a loss.

"The human heart harbours evil. . . ."

"That's quite enough — the same nonsense!" Nu-wa flushed with anger from her cheeks to her ears. Wheeling round, she searched till she found a small creature devoid of metal strips, naked and covered with wounds which were still bleeding. He hastily fastened round his loins a ragged cloth just stripped from one of his fellows, now stiff and stark. He retained his self-possession, however, throughout.

Imagining that he belonged to a different species from the others and would be able to tell her something, Nu-wa asked:

"What happened?"

"What happened?" He raised his head slightly.

"That accident just now. . . ."

"That accident just now? . . ."

"Was it a war?" She was reduced to guessing.

"A war?" He repeated her question.

Nu-wa inhaled a mouthful of cold air and looked up at the sky. There was a great crack across it, deep and wide. Nu-wa stood up and tapped the sky with her fingers. Instead of a clear ring, it gave a sound like a cracked bowl. With wrinkled brows she looked round and reflected before wringing the water out of her hair, throwing it back over both shoulders and starting with fresh energy to gather reeds. She had made up her mind to mend the sky before doing anything else.

Day after day, night after night, she piled up reeds. But as the pile grew in height, Nu-wa lost weight, for things were very different now. Above was the sky with jagged crack, below the earth slimy and gutted — there was nothing to rejoice her eyes or her heart.

When the pile of reeds reached the crack, she looked for blue stones. Her original plan was to use stones the same pure blue as the sky, but there were not enough of these and she shrank from using the mountains. When she searched for fragments in the places humming with life, she met with jeers or curses. Some little creatures dragged away what she had found or even bit her fingers. She was reduced then to mixing in some white stones. When she ran out of these, she made do with red, yellow or grey. At last the crack was filled up. She had only to light the fire to melt the stones and her task would be done. But her eyes were seeing stars, her ears buzzing from exhaustion. She was at the end of her strength.

"Dear me, I've never felt so low in my life." She sat on a hill-top to rest her head on her hands. Her breath was coming in gasps.

The great fire in the primeval forests on Mount Kunlun was still ablaze, incarnadining the whole western horizon. A glance in that direction decided her to take a big burning tree from there to light her heap of reeds. Before she could reach out, something pricked her foot.

She looked down at one of the small creatures she had made, even stranger than the others. From head to foot he was hung with thick folds of drapery, with a dozen or more supernumerary ribbons at his waist. He had a covering of some sort on his head, crowned by a small black oblong board. In his hands was a tablet which had pricked her foot.

This creature crowned with the oblong board stood between Nu-wa's legs and looked up at her. When her glance fell on him, he made haste to present the tablet, which she took. It was a highly polished green bamboo tablet on which were two columns of minute black specks, far smaller than those on oak leaves. Nu-wa admired the skilful craftsmanship.

"What's this?" she could not help asking curiously.

The creature crowned with the oblong board indicated the bamboo tablet and recited glibly:

"Your lewd nakedness is immoral, an offence against etiquette, a breach of the rules and conduct fit for beasts! This is forbidden by the laws of the land!"

Nu-wa stared at the oblong board, secretly amused by her own folly in asking such a question. She should have known by now that she could have no real communication with these creatures. Without another word, she put the bamboo tablet on the oblong board. Then from the forest she plucked a great burning tree to set light to her pile of reeds.

Suddenly she heard sobs, a strange new sound to her. She glanced down. In the little eyes beneath the board were two tiny tears even smaller than mustard seeds. Since this was totally unlike the cries "nga nga" she had heard before, she did not realize that this was another form of weeping.

She set about lighting the fire in several places.

It burned slowly at first because the reeds were still damp. It made a great roar none the less, and after some time countless tongues of flame shot out, flickering up to lick all above. Some time later they formed a double flower of flame, a pillar of fire of a scarlet much more intense than the red glow on Mount Kunlun. A high wind sprang up, the fiery pillar whirled and roared, the blue stones and the stones of many colours became a uniform crimson. They rushed into the crack like a torrent of melted sugar or unflickering sheet lightning.

The wind and the heat of the fire tossed her hair in all directions. Sweat was coursing off her like a waterfall. The dazzling flames lit up her body. For the last time the universe was a flesh pink.

By degrees the pillar of fire rose, leaving nothing but a heap of ashes beneath. When the sky was blue again she reached out to finger it, and felt a number of irregularities.

"When I'm strong again, I'll have another try . . ." she thought.

She bent down to pick up the ashes of the reeds and dropped them into the flooded parts of the earth. Still hot, the ashes made the water boil and water and ashes splashed over her. The wind would not stop either, but buffeted her with ashes till she was grey.

With a faint sigh she breathed her last.

In the blood-red clouds at the horizon was the glorious sun like some fluid orb of gold lapped in a waste of ancient lava. Opposite, the frigid white moon seemed as if made of iron. It was hard to say which was setting or which rising. Utterly spent, Nu-wa fell back between them, no longer breathing.

On every side, high and low, reigned a silence deeper than death.

III

One bitterly cold day a vague tumult could be heard. The royal troops had fought their way to this spot. They came late, having waited for the flames and dust to subside. To the left, a yellow axe. To the right, a black axe. Behind, a huge, ancient standard. Warily, ready to turn and flee, they advanced to where the corpse of Nu-wa lay, but observed no sign of life. The soldiers encamped on her stomach, since that was a fertile spot — they were shrewd in such choices. Then abruptly changing their tune, they announced that they were the true descendants of the goddess and altered the tadpole-shaped characters on their standard to: "The Entrails of Nu-wa."

The old priest left stranded on the beach taught countless generations of disciples. Not till the hour of his death did he reveal to one of them the important news that the Fairy Mountains had been carried out to sea by the giant tortoises. This disciple in turn told his own disciples, till finally an alchemist, hoping to win favour, informed the First Emperor of Chin, who sent him off on a search.[1]

The alchemist failed to find the Fairy Islands, and eventually the First Emperor of Chin died. Emperor Wu[2] of Han sent out search parties too, but they were no more successful.

Very likely the giant tortoises had not grasped Nu-wa's meaning and the fact that they nodded was sheer coincidence. After carelessly carrying the mountains for a while they submerged to sleep, and the mountains sank after them. That is why, to this day, no one has seen so much as a sign of the Fairy Isles. All they have discovered are a few islands inhabited by barbarians.

November 1922

---

[1] The First Emperor of Chin (246-210 B.C.) sent the alchemist Hsu Fu with several thousand people out to sea to look for the fairy islands.

[2] 140-87 B.C.

The Flight to the Moon

I

It is a fact that intelligent beasts can divine the wishes of men. As soon as their gate came in sight the horse slowed down and, hanging its head at the same moment as its rider, let it jog with each step like a pestle pounding rice.

The great house was overhung with evening mist, while thick black smoke rose from the neighbours' chimneys. It was time for supper. At the sound of hoofs, retainers had come out and were standing erect with their arms at their sides before the entrance. As Yi[1] dismounted listlessly beside the rubbish heap, they stepped forward to relieve him of his reins and whip. At the moment of crossing the threshold, he looked down at the quiverful of brand-new arrows at his waist and the three crows and one shattered sparrow in his bag, and his heart sank within him. But he strode in, putting a bold face on things, the arrows rattling in his quiver.

Reaching the inner courtyard, he saw Chang-ngo[2] looking out from the round window. He knew her sharp eyes

---

[1] Yi or Hou Yi was a heroic archer in ancient Chinese legends.

[2] A goddess in ancient Chinese mythology, supposed to be Yi's wife. She took some drug of immortality and flew to the moon to become a goddess there.

must have seen the crows, and in dismay he came to a sudden stop — but he had to go on in. Serving-maids came out to greet him, unfastened his bow and quiver and took his game bag. He noticed that their smiles were rather forced.

After wiping his face and hands he entered the inner apartment, calling: "Madam. . . ."

Chang-ngo had been watching the sunset from the round window. She turned slowly and threw him an indifferent glance without returning his greeting.

He had been used to this treatment for some time, for over a year at least. But as usual he went on in and sat down on the old, worn leopard skin over the wooden couch opposite. Scratching his head, he muttered:

"I was out of luck again today. Nothing but crows. . . ."

"Pah!"

Raising her willowy eyebrows, Chang-ngo sprang up and swept from the room, grumbling as she went: "Noodles with crow sauce again! Noodles with crow sauce again! I'd like to know who else eats nothing but noodles with crow sauce from one year to the next? How ill-fated I was to marry you and eat noodles with crow sauce the whole year round!"

"Madam!" Yi leaped to his feet and followed her. "It wasn't so bad today," he continued softly. "I shot a sparrow too, which can be dressed for you. . . . Nu-hsin!" he called to the maid. "Bring that sparrow to show your mistress."

The game had been taken to the kitchen, but Nu-hsin ran to fetch the sparrow and held it out in both hands to Chang-ngo.

"That!" With a disdainful glance she reached slowly out to touch it. "How disgusting!" she said crossly. "You've smashed it to pieces! Where's the meat?"

17

"I know," admitted Yi, discomfited. "My bow is too powerful, my arrow-heads are too large."

"Can't you use smaller arrows?"

"I haven't any. When I shot the giant boar and the huge python. . . ."

"Is this a giant boar or a huge python?" She turned to Nu-hsin and ordered: "Use it for soup!" Then she went back to her room.

Left alone at a loss, Yi sat down with his back to the wall to listen to the crackling of firewood in the kitchen. He remembered the bulk of the giant boar which had loomed like a small hillock in the distance. If he hadn't shot it then but left it till now, it would have kept them in meat for half a year and spared them this daily worry about food. And the huge python! What soups it could have made!

Nu-yi lit the lamp. The vermilion bow and arrows, the black bow and arrows, the crossbow, the sword and the dagger glimmered on the opposite wall in its faint rays. After one look, Yi lowered his head and sighed. Nu-hsin brought supper in and set it on the table in the middle: five large bowls of noodles on the left, two large bowls of noodles and one of soup on the right, in the centre one large bowl of crow sauce.

While eating, Yi had to admit that this was not an appetizing meal. He stole a glance at Chang-ngo. Without so much as looking at the crow sauce, she had steeped her noodles in soup, and she set down her bowl half finished. Her face struck him as paler and thinner than before — suppose she were to fall ill?

By the second watch, in a slightly better mood, she sat without a word on the edge of the bed to drink some water. Yi sat on the wooden couch next to her, stroking the old leopard skin which was losing its fur.

"Ah," he said in a conciliatory tone. "I bagged this spotted leopard on the Western Hill before we married. It was a beauty — one glossy mass of gold."

That reminded him of how they had lived in the old days. Of bears they ate nothing but the paws, of camels nothing but the hump, giving all the rest to the serving-maids and retainers. When the big game was finished they ate wild boars, rabbits and pheasants. He was such a fine archer, he could shoot as much as he pleased.

A sigh escaped him.

"The fact is I'm too good a shot," he said. "That's why the whole place is cleaned out. Who could have guessed we'd be left with nothing but crows?"

Chang-ngo gave the ghost of a smile.

"Today I was luckier than usual." Yi's spirits were rising. "At least I caught a sparrow. I had to go an extra thirty *li* to find it."

"Can't you go a little further still?"

"Yes, madam. That's what I mean to do. I'll get up earlier tomorrow morning. If you wake first, call me. I mean to go fifty *li* further to see if I can't find some roe-bucks or rabbits. . . . It won't be easy, though. Remember all the game there was when I shot the giant boar and the huge python? Black bears used to pass in front of your mother's door, and she asked me several times to shoot them. . . ."

"Really?" It seemed to have slipped Chang-ngo's memory.

"Who could have foreseen they would all disappear like this? Come to think of it, I don't know how we're going to manage. *I'm* all right. I've only to eat that elixir the priest gave me, and I can fly up to heaven. But I must think of you first . . . that's why I've decided to go a little further tomorrow. . . ."

"Um."

Chang-ngo had finished the water. She lay down slowly and closed her eyes.

The lamp, burning low, lit up her fading make-up. Much of her powder had rubbed off, there were dark circles beneath her eyes and one of her eyebrows was blacker than the other; still her mouth was as red as fire, and though she wasn't smiling you could see faint dimples on her cheeks.

"Ah, no! How can I feed a woman like this on nothing but noodles and crow sauce!"

Overcome by shame, Yi flushed up to his ears.

II

Night passed, a new day dawned.

In a flash Yi opened his eyes. A sunbeam aslant the western wall told him it could not be early. He looked at Chang-ngo, who was lying stretched out fast asleep. Without a sound he threw on his clothes, slipped down from his leopard skin couch and tiptoed into the hall. As he washed his face he told Nu-keng to order Wang Sheng to saddle his horse.

Having so much to do, he had long since given up breakfast. Nu-yi put five baked cakes, five stalks of leek and a package of paprika in his game bag, fastening this firmly to his waist with his bow and arrows. He tightened his belt and strode lightly out of the hall, telling Nu-keng whom he met:

"I mean to go further today to look for game. I may be a little late back. When your mistress has had her breakfast and is in good spirits, give her my apologies and ask her to wait for me for supper. Don't forget — my apologies!"

He walked swiftly out, swung into the saddle and flashed past the retainers ranged on either side. Very soon he was out of the village. In front were the *kaoliang* fields through which he passed every day. These he ignored, having learned long ago that there was nothing here. With two cracks of his whip he galloped forward, covering sixty *li* without a pause. In front was a dense forest, and since his horse was winded and in a lather it naturally slowed down. Another ten *li* and they were in the forest, yet Yi could see nothing but wasps, butterflies, ants and locusts — not a trace of birds or beasts. The first sight of this unexplored territory had raised hopes of catching at least a couple of foxes or rabbits but now he knew that had been an idle dream. He made his way out and saw another stretch of green *kaoliang* fields ahead, with one or two mud cottages in the distance. The breeze was balmy, the sun warm; neither crow nor sparrow could be heard.

"Confound it!" he bellowed to relieve his feelings.

A dozen paces further on, however, and his heart leaped with joy. On the flat ground outside a mud hut in the distance there was actually a fowl. Stopping to peck at every step, it looked like a large pigeon. He seized his bow and fitted an arrow to it, drew it to its full extent and then let go. His shaft sped through the air like a shooting star.

With no hesitation, for he never missed his quarry, he spurred after the arrow to retrieve the game. But as he approached it an old woman hurried towards the horse. She had picked up the large pigeon transfixed by his arrow and was shouting:

"Who are you? Why have you shot my best black laying hen? Have you nothing better to do? . . ."

Yi's heart missed a beat. He pulled up short.

"What! A hen?" he echoed nervously. "I thought it was a wood pigeon."

"Are you blind? You must be over forty too."

"Yes, ma'am. Forty-five last year."

"No fool like an old fool, they say. Imagine mistaking a hen for a wood pigeon! Who are you anyway?"

"I am Yi." While saying this he saw that his arrow had pierced the hen's heart, killing it outright. So his voice trailed away on his name as he dismounted.

"Yi? . . . Never heard of him!" She peered into his face.

"There are those who know my name. In the days of good King Yao I shot wild boars and serpents. . . ."

"Oh, you liar! Those were shot by Lord Feng Meng[1] and some others. Maybe you helped. But how can you boast of doing it all yourself? For shame!"

"Why, ma'am, that fellow Feng Meng has just taken to calling on me during the last few years. We never worked together. He had no part in it."

"Liar! Everybody says so. I hear it four or five times a month."

"All right. Let's come down to business. What about this hen?"

"You must make it up! She was my best: she laid me an egg every day. You'll have to give me two hoes and three spindles in exchange."

"Look at me, ma'am — I neither farm nor spin. Where would I get hoes or spindles? I've no money on me either, only five baked cakes — but they're made of white flour. I'll give you these for your hen with five stalks of leek and a package of paprika into the bargain. What do you say? . . ."

---

[1] Yi's pupil and another good archer. This is a thrust at Kao Chang-hung, a young writer who was Lu Hsun's pupil but later attacked him in his articles. The story of Feng Meng shooting Yi suggests Kao's attack on Lu Hsun.

Taking the cakes from his bag with one hand, he picked up the hen with the other.

The old woman was not averse to taking cakes of white flour, but insisted on having fifteen. After haggling for some time they agreed on ten, and Yi promised to bring the rest over by noon the next day at the latest, leaving the arrow there as security. Then, his mind at rest, he stuffed the dead hen in his bag, sprang into his saddle and headed home. Though famished, he was happy. It was over a year since they last tasted chicken soup.

It was afternoon when he emerged from the forest, and he plied his whip hard in his eagerness to get home. His horse was exhausted, though, and not till dusk did they reach the familiar *kaoliang* fields. He glimpsed a shadowy figure some way off, and almost at once an arrow sang through the air towards him.

Without reining in his horse, which was trotting along, Yi fitted an arrow to his bow and let fly. Zing! Two arrow-heads collided, sparks flew into the air and the two shafts thrust up to form an inverted V before toppling over and falling to the ground. No sooner had the first two met than both men loosed their second, which collided again in mid-air. They did this nine times, till Yi's supply was exhausted; and now he could see Feng Meng opposite, gloating as he aimed another arrow at his throat.

"Well, well!" thought Yi. "I imagined he was fishing at the seaside, but he's been hanging about to play dirty tricks like this. Now I understand the old woman talking as she did. . . ."

In a flash, his enemy's bow arched like a full moon and the arrow whistled through the air towards Yi's throat. Perhaps the aim was at fault, for it struck him full in the mouth. He tumbled over, transfixed, and fell to the ground. His horse stood motionless.

Seeing Yi was dead, Feng Meng tiptoed slowly over. Smiling as if drinking to his victory, he gazed at the corpse's face.

He stared long and hard till Yi opened his eyes and sat up.

"You've learned nothing in a hundred visits or more to me." He spat out the arrow and laughed. "Don't you know my skill in 'biting the arrow'? That's too bad! These tricks of yours won't get you anywhere. You can't kill your boxing master with blows learned from him. You must work out something of your own."

"I was trying to 'pay you out in your own coin' . . ." mumbled the victor.

Yi stood up, laughing heartily. "You're always quoting some adage. Maybe you can impress old women that way, but you can't impose on *me*. I've always stuck to hunting, never taken to highway robbery like you. . . ."

Relieved to see that the hen in his bag was not crushed, he remounted and rode away.

"Curse you. . . ." An oath carried after him.

"To think he should stoop so low. . . . Such a young fellow, and yet he's picked up swearing. No wonder that old woman was taken in."

Yi shook his head sadly as he rode along.

III

Before he came to the end of the *kaoliang* fields, night fell. Stars appeared in the dark blue sky, and the evening star shone with unusual brilliance in the west. The horse picked its way along the white ridges between the fields, so weary that its pace was slower than ever. Fortunately, at the horizon the moon began to shed its silver light.

"Confound it!" Yi, whose belly was rumbling now, lost patience. "The harder I try to make a living, the more tiresome things happen to waste my time." He spurred his horse, but it simply twitched its rump and jogged on as slowly as before.

"Chang-ngo is sure to be angry," he thought. "It's so late! She may fly into a temper. Thank goodness I've this little hen to make her happy. I'll tell her: 'Madam, I went two hundred *li* there and back to find you this.' No, that's no good: sounds too boastful."

Now to his joy he saw lights ahead and stopped worrying. And without any urging the horse broke into a canter. A round, snow-white moon lit up the path before him and a cool wind soothed his cheeks — this was better than coming home from a great hunt!

The horse stopped of its own accord beside the rubbish heap. Yi saw at a glance that something was amiss. The whole house was in confusion. Chao Fu alone came out to meet him.

"What's happened? Where's Wang Sheng?" he demanded.

"He's gone to the Yao family to look for our mistress."

"What? Has your mistress gone to the Yao family?" Yi was too taken aback to dismount.

"Yes, sir." Chao took the reins and whip.

Then Yi got down from his horse and crossed the threshold. After a moment's thought he turned to ask:

"Are you sure she didn't grow tired of waiting and go to a restaurant?"

"No, sir. I've asked in all three restaurants. She isn't there."

His head lowered in thought, Yi entered the house. The three maids were standing nervously in front of the hall. He cried out in amazement:

"What! All of you here? Your mistress never goes alone to the Yao family."

They looked at him in silence, then took off his bow, the quiver and the bag holding the small hen. Yi had a moment of panic. Suppose Chang-ngo had killed herself in anger? He sent Nu-keng for Chao Fu, and told him to search the pond in the back and the trees. Once in their room, though, he knew his guess had been wrong. The place was in utter disorder, all the chests were open and one glance behind the bed showed that the jewel-case was missing. He felt as if doused with cold water. Gold and pearls meant nothing to him, but the elixir given him by the priest had been in that case too.

After walking twice round the room, he noticed Wang Sheng at the door.

"Please, sir, our mistress isn't with the Yaos. They're not playing mah-jong today."

Yi looked at him and said nothing. Wang Sheng withdrew.

"Did you call me, sir?" asked Chao Fu, coming in.

Yi shook his head and waved him away.

He walked round and round the room, then went to the hall and sat down. Looking up he could see on the opposite wall the vermilion bow and arrows, the black bow and arrows, the crossbow, the sword and the dagger. After some reflection, he asked the maids who were standing there woodenly:

"What time did your mistress disappear?"

"She wasn't here when I brought in the lamp," said Nu-yi. "But no one saw her go out."

"Did you see her take the medicine in that case?"

"No, sir. But she did ask me for some water this afternoon."

Yi stood up in consternation. He suspected that he had been left alone on earth!

"Did you see anything flying to heaven?" he asked.

"Oh!" Nu-hsin was struck by a thought. "When I came out after lighting the lamp, I did see a black shadow flying this way. I never dreamed it was our mistress. . . ." Her face turned pale.

"It must have been!" Yi clapped his knee and sprang up. He started out, turning back to ask Nu-hsin: "Which way did the shadow go?"

Nu-hsin pointed with one finger. But all he could see in that direction was the round, snow-white moon suspended in the sky, with its hazy pavilions and trees. When he was a child his grandmother had told him of the lovely landscape of the moon; he still had a vague recollection of her description. As he watched the moon floating in a sapphire sea, his own limbs seemed very heavy.

Fury took possession of him. And in his fury he felt the urge to kill. With eyes starting from his head, he roared at the maids:

"Bring my bow! The one with which I shot the suns! And three arrows!"

Nu-yi and Nu-keng took down the huge bow in the middle of the hall and dusted it. They handed it to him with three long arrows.

Holding the bow in one hand, with the other he fitted the three arrows to the string. He drew the bow to the full, aiming straight at the moon. Standing there firm as a rock, his eyes darting lightning, his beard and hair flying in the wind like black tongues of flame, for one instant he looked again the hero who had long ago shot the suns.

A whistling was heard, one only. The three shafts left the string, one after the other, too fast for eye to see or ear to hear. They should have struck the moon in the same place, for they followed each other without a hair's breadth between them. But to be sure of reaching his mark he had given each a slightly different direction, so that the arrows struck three different points, inflicting three wounds.

The maids gave a cry. They saw the moon quiver and thought it must surely fall — but still it hung there peacefully, shedding a calm, even brighter light, as if completely unscathed.

Yi threw back his head to hurl an oath at the sky. He watched and waited. But the moon paid no attention. He took three paces forward, and the moon fell back three paces. He took three paces back, and the moon moved forward.

They looked at each other in silence.

Listlessly, he leaned his bow against the door of the hall. He went inside. The maids followed him.

He sat down and sighed. "Well, your mistress will be happy on her own for ever after. How could she have the heart to leave me and fly up there alone? Did she find me too old? But only last month she said: 'You're not old. It's a sign of mental weakness to think of yourself as old. . . .'"

"That couldn't be it," said Nu-yi. "Folk still describe you as a warrior, sir."

"Sometimes you seem like an artist," put in Nu-hsin.

"Nonsense! The fact is, those noodles with crow sauce were uneatable. I can't blame her for not being able to stomach them. . . ."

"That leopard skin is worn out on one side. I'll cut a piece of the leg facing the wall to mend it. That will look better." Nu-hsin walked inside.

"Wait a bit!" said Yi and reflected. "There's no hurry for that. I'm famished. Make haste and cook me a dish of chicken with paprika, and make five catties of flapjacks. After that I can go to bed. Tomorrow I'm going to ask that priest for another elixir, so that I can follow her. Tell Wang Sheng, Nu-keng, to give my horse four measures of beans!"

December 1926

Curbing the Flood

I

This was the time when "the Great Flood brought devastation, encircling mountains and engulfing hills."[1] Not all the subjects of Emperor Shun flocked on to the heights still above the water. Some tied themselves to tree tops, some took to rafts, on a number of which they rigged up tiny plank shelters — a thoroughly poetic sight seen from the cliffs.

News from distant parts was brought by raft. Eventually everyone knew that Lord Kun,[2] who had grappled with the flood for nine years to no effect, had incurred the imperial displeasure and been exiled to the Feather Mountain. He had apparently been succeeded by his son, young Lord Wen-ming, whose milk name was Ah Yu.[3]

So long was the land flooded that the universities closed and there was no space even for kindergartens, with the result that the common people became rather muddle-

---

[1] A quotation from the *Book of History*, a collection from the early dynasties.

[2] Lord Kun failed to curb the flood and was killed in the Feather Mountain.

[3] Yu was supposed to be Kun's son. Because he was successful in curbing the flood he succeeded Shun as emperor.

headed. Many scholars had assembled on the Mount of Culture,[1] however. Since food was brought to them by flying chariot from the Kingdom of Marvellous Artisans, they need fear no want and could pursue their studies. Yet most of them were opposed to Yu or questioned his very existence.

Once a month a whirring and chugging in mid-air grew louder and louder till the flying chariot hove in sight. The gold circle on its flag emitted a faint effulgence. Five feet

---

[1] This interlude about the scholars assembled on the Mount of Culture is a satire on some cultural figures and a few reactionary scholars at the time of the Second Revolutionary Civil War. The name "Mount of Culture" is an allusion to what had happened in October 1932 when more than thirty cultural figures in Peking including Chiang Han, Liu Fu, Hsu Ping-chang and Ma Heng petitioned the Kuomintang government to declare Peking a "city of culture." At that time the Japanese imperialists had occupied the northeastern provinces, and north China was in a precarious position. The Kuomintang government, following a policy of surrendering and selling the country to the enemy, was preparing to withdraw from the north and to move ancient relics which could be sold from Peking to Nanking. Chiang Han and the others tried to stop the removal of these ancient cultural treasures, but they claimed that Peking had no political nor military importance and made the fantastic proposal that the government should stop defending Peking, declaring it a cultural zone. So they requested "the government to declare Peiping a city of culture, moving all military institutions to Paoting." It is very clear that this proposal was not only fallacious, but that it coincided with the plot of Japanese imperialism at that time and also echoed the "argument" of the Kuomintang government with its policy of capitulation. Though the Kuomintang government did not declare Peking a "city of culture," it did eventually surrender Peking to the Japanese imperialists, while most of the cultural relics were taken to Nanking early in 1933. Lu Hsun from the time of the Japanese imperialists' occupation of Shenyang on September 18, 1931 to his death, wrote many articles exposing the Kuomintang government's betrayal of the nation and in one of his essays he attacked this proposal for a "city of culture." Here he is ridiculing the fallacious arguments used by Chiang Han and the others in their petition; while some of the "scholars" are clearly modelled on contemporary figures who held reactionary views.

31

from the ground, it would let down baskets the contents of which were known to none but the scholars. Conversations like this were carried on vertically:

"Good morning!"[1]

"How do you do?"

"Glu. . . . Gli. . . ."

"O.K."

After this the flying chariot flew swiftly back to the Kingdom of Marvellous Artisans, there was not a sound in the sky and the scholars fell silent too — they were busy eating. All that could be heard was the pounding of breakers against the mountain boulders. Then, energy restored by a siesta, academic discussions drowned the sound of the waves.

"Yu will never succeed in curbing the flood, not if he's the son of Kun," declared a scholar who walked with a cane. "I have collected the genealogies of many kings, dukes, ministers and rich families. Long and careful study has led me to this conclusion: all the descendants of the rich are rich, all those of the wicked are wicked — this is known as 'heredity.' It follows that, if Kun was unsuccessful, Yu will inevitably be unsuccessful too; for fools cannot give birth to wise men!"

"O.K.," agreed a scholar without a cane.

"But think of His Majesty's father!" put in another scholar without a cane.

"He may have been a little 'dull,' but he has improved. Your true fool can never improve. . . ."

"O.K."

"Th — that's all n — n — nonsense!" stuttered another scholar, his nose promptly turning red. "You've been led astray by rumours. As a matter of fact, there is no such

---

[1] This dialogue is given in English in the original to parody certain Westernized pseudo-scholars.

person as Yu. Yu is a reptile. Can a r — reptile curb the flood? Kun doesn't exist either. Kun is a fish. Can a f — fish curb the fl — fl — flood?" He stamped both feet vehemently.

"There's no question of Kun's existence. Seven years ago I saw him with my own eyes when he went to the foot of Mount Kunlun to enjoy the plum blossom."

"In that case, there must be some mistake over the name. He should be called Man, not Kun. As for Yu, I assure you he's a reptile. I have copious evidence to prove his non-existence. You may judge for yourselves. . . ."

He rose boldly to his feet, produced a knife and started peeling the bark from five great pines. Making a paste of some left-over bread-crumbs and water, he mixed this with charcoal to write on the trees in minute tadpole-shaped characters his arguments proving that Yu had never existed. He wrote for three times nine — twenty-seven — whole days. All who wanted to read this thesis had to pay ten succulent elm leaves or, if they lived on rafts, a shellful of fresh duckweed.

Water was everywhere, making it impossible to hunt or farm. The survivors had so much time on their hands that many came to read. After a crowd had milled round the pines for three days, sighs of admiration and exhaustion could be heard on all sides. But on the fourth day at noon, when the scholar was eating fried noodles, a peasant spoke up:

"There *are* men called Yu. And Yu doesn't mean 'reptile.' It's our country fashion of writing the 'Yu' for ape."

"Are there men c — called Ape? . . ." roared the scholar, leaping to his feet and gulping down a half-chewed mouthful of noodles. His nose had turned a bright purple.

"Of course there are. Why, I know some called Dog and Cat too!"

"Don't argue with him. Mr. Bird-Head," interposed the scholar with the cane, putting down his bread. "All these country folk are fools. Bring me your genealogy!" he shouted at the villager. "I shall prove beyond a doubt that all your forbears were fools. . . ."

"I've never had a genealogy. . . ."

"Bah! It's disgusting types like this who make accuracy impossible in my researches!"

"But for this you don't need a gen — genealogy. My theory can't be wrong." Mr. Bird-Head sounded even more outraged. "Many scholars have written to me expressing approval. I've got all their letters here. . . ."

"No, no, we ought to refer to his genealogy. . . ."

"But I haven't any genealogy," said the "fool." "And in troubled times like these, cut off as we are, to get proof in the form of letters of approval from your friends will be more difficult than performing a religious service in a snail-shell. The proof is here before us: your name is Mr. Bird-Head. Are you really a bird's head instead of a man?"

"Confound it!" Mr. Bird-Head flushed purple to the ears with fury. "How dare you insult me! Insinuating that I'm not a man! Let's go to Lord Kao Yao[1] and settle our difference by law! If I'm not a man, I'll gladly undergo capital punishment — in other words, I'll have my head cut off. Understand? If not, you'll be punished instead. Just you wait! Don't move till I've finished my noodles."

"Sir," replied the villager stolidly, "as a learned man you ought to know that it is after noon now and other people are hungry too. The trouble is that fools have the same stomach as wise men — they get hungry just the same. I'm very sorry, but I must go and fish for duckweed.

---

[1] Legendary minister of justice in ancient China, under the sage Emperor Shun.

I'll come to court when you've filed your complaint."
With that he jumped on to his raft, picked up his net and
drifted off to gather water-weeds. One by one, the other
spectators scattered too, leaving Mr. Bird-Head with a
scarlet nose and ears to make a fresh start on his noodles,
while the scholar with the cane shook his head.

But was Yu really a reptile or a man? This major issue
remained unsettled.

II

Yu did seem to be a reptile after all.

Over half a year had passed, the flying chariot from
the Kingdom of Marvellous Artisans had come eight times,
and nine out of ten of the raft-dwellers who had read the
writing on the pines had beriberi; but there was still no
word of the new official charged with curbing the flood.
Not till the flying chariot had paid its tenth visit did it
become known that there was indeed a man named Yu,
that he was indeed the son of Kun and the imperially ap-
pointed Minister of Water Conservancy, that he had left
Chichou[1] three years earlier and might arrive at any time.

Though mildly excited, all remained cool and sceptical.
They had heard so many unreliable rumours of the sort
before that they tended to turn a deaf ear to all such talk.

This time, though, the news did seem to be well-founded.
A fortnight later, everybody was saying that the minister
would arrive very soon. For a man out collecting floating
weeds had seen the official boats. Indeed he could show
a black and blue bump on his head which he explained
had been caused by a stone thrown by a guard when he

---

[1] One of the nine ancient Chinese provinces. According to legend
the curbing of the flood began in Chichou.

did not get out of the way quickly enough. Here was palpable evidence of the minister's arrival. This man promptly became exceedingly famous and busy. Everyone rushed to look at the bump on his head, nearly swamping his raft in the process. Then the scholars summoned him and decided after serious research that his bump was a genuine bump. This forced Mr. Bird-Head to relinquish his views and he made over·historical studies to others while he went off to collect folk ballads.

A flotilla of large boats, each made from a single tree, arrived about twenty days after the bump was raised. On each boat twenty guards were pulling at the oars, thirty guards were holding lances. At both stem and stern were flags. As soon as this fleet reached the mountain top, it received a respectful welcome from a band of local gentry and scholars on the bank. After some time, from the largest vessel emerged two middle-aged, corpulent officials, escorted by a score or so of soldiers in tiger skins. They made their way, with those who had welcomed them, to the stone building on the highest peak.

On dry land as well as on the water, folk craned their necks to catch what was being said and learned that these were two government inspectors, not Yu himself.

The officials seated themselves in the centre of the building and, after eating some bread, began their investigation.

"The situation is not too desperate. There is just about enough to eat." A specialist in the Miao dialect was spokesman for the scholars. "Bread is dropped once a month from mid-air and there is no lack of fish which, though inevitably tasting of mud, is very fat, Your Honours. As for the lower orders, they have plenty of elm leaves and seaweed. They 'eat all day without exerting their minds' — in other words, since they do not have to use their heads what they have is quite enough.

We've tasted their food and it is not unpleasant, with quite a distinctive flavour. . . ."

"Besides," put in another scholar, an expert on the *Materia Medica* of Emperor Shen Nung,[1] "there is Vitamin W in elm leaves, and iodine which cures scrofula in seaweed — both thoroughly nutritious."

"O.K.," said another scholar. The officials stared at him in surprise.

"As for drink, they have all they want," went on the expert. "More than enough to last ten thousand generations. Unfortunately it is mixed with a little mud so that distillation is necessary before drinking. But though I have pointed this out time and again, they are too pig-headed to carry out instructions; hence countless are ill. . . ."

"Aren't they to blame for the flood too?" interposed a gentleman in a long dark brown gown, his beard clipped to five points. "Before the flood came, they were too lazy to repair the dykes. When the flood came, they were too lazy to drain it off. . . ."

"That's what's called the loss of spiritual values," chuckled an essayist in the style of the time of Fu Hsi,[2] a man with pointed moustaches who was seated in the back row. "When I climbed the Pamirs the winds of heaven were blowing, the plum was in flower, white clouds were sailing past, the price of gold was mounting, the rats were sleeping. I saw a youth with a cigar in his mouth and on his face the mist of Chih Yu[3]. . . . Ha, ha, ha! It can't be helped. . . ."

---

[1] The most ancient Chinese book on medical herbs. The date of its compilation is uncertain, but it is probably written in the Han or Wei Dynasty and attributed to Shen Nung.

[2] A legendary emperor in ancient China said to have invented the trigrams.

[3] Chih Yu according to ancient legend was the chief of the Chiu-li tribe in the north.

"O.K."

Talk in this vein went on for hours. The officials, having listened attentively, finally told them to draw up a joint report, preferably with detailed proposals for rehabilitation. With this, the officials boarded their boat again.

The next day, on the pretext of exhaustion from the voyage, they transacted no business and received no visitors. The third day, the scholars invited them to see the umbrella-shaped old pine on the highest peak, while in the afternoon they went to fish for yellow eels behind the mountain, enjoying themselves till dusk. The fourth day, on the pretext of exhaustion from inspection, they transacted no business and received no visitors. On the fifth day, after noon, they sent for the spokesman of the lower orders.

The lower orders had started choosing a spokesman four days previously, but nobody would undertake the task, all pleading their complete ignorance of officials. Thereupon the man with the bump on his head was elected by a majority, since he had some knowledge of the official world. At this his bump, which had subsided, started twinging as if being pricked by a needle. With tears in his eyes he swore: "Death is better than being a spokesman!" The others crowded round day and night to urge upon him his moral obligations. They accused him of neglecting the public interest, of being a selfish individualist who should not be suffered to remain in China. The more impassioned shook their fists in his face, holding him responsible for the flood. Nearly dropping with fatigue, he decided that to sacrifice himself for the common good would be better than being hounded to death on the raft. Making supreme effort of will, on the fourth day he agreed.

He was acclaimed by the crowd. But by then a few bold spirits felt a twinge of envy.

At dawn on the fifth day, the others dragged him to the river bank to wait for a summons. Sure enough, the officials summoned him. His legs shook beneath him, but once more he made a supreme effort of will. Then, after two great yawns, with puffy eyes, feeling as if he had left the ground and were treading on air, he boarded the official boat.

Strange to relate, neither the guards with lances nor the warriors in tiger skins beat him or swore at him — they let him pass into the central cabin. There bear-skins and leopard-skins strewed the floor, bows and arrows hung from the walls, and the vases and pots on all sides quite dazzled his eyes. Pulling himself together, he saw seated in the place of honour opposite two corpulent officials. He dared not look too closely at their faces.

"Are you the spokesman of the common people?" asked one of the officials.

"They sent me here." His eyes were fixed on the spots like mugwort leaves on the leopard-skins on the floor.

"How are things with you?"

Not understanding, he made no reply.

"Are you doing all right?"

"Yes, thanks to Your Honours' goodness. . . ." After a moment's thought, he added softly: "We make do. . . . We're muddling through. . . ."

"What are you eating?"

"Leaves, water-weed. . . ."

"Can you eat such things?"

"Oh yes, we're used to anything. We can eat anything. Only some young scamps make a song and dance about it. The human heart is growing evil, devil take it! But we give them a good thrashing!"

The officials laughed and one said to the other: "An honest fellow!"

This praise went to the fellow's head, emboldening him to give vent to a torrent of words:

"We can always think of some way out. Water-weed, now, is best made into Slippery Emerald Soup, while elm leaves make good First-at-Court Gruel. We don't strip all the bark from the trees, but leave some so that next spring there'll be new leaves on the boughs for us to pick. If, thanks to Your Honours' kindness, we could catch eels. . . ."

The officials seemed to have lost interest, however, for one of them gave two huge yawns one after another, then put in sharply: "Draw up a joint report, preferably with detailed proposals for rehabilitation."

"But none of us can write!" he said timidly.

"Are you all illiterate? This is really very backward of you! In that case, bring us one sample of everything you eat."

Having left fearfully yet jubilantly, rubbing his bump, he lost no time in transmitting the officials' orders to the dwellers on the shore, the trees and the rafts. Moreover he ordered them loudly: "This is for the higher-ups! All must be done cleanly, carefully and handsomely. . . ."

Together the common people set to work to wash leaves, cut bark and collect water-weed — all was bustle and confusion. He himself planed wood for a casket in which to present their offerings. Having polished two planks of wood till they shone, he hurried that same night to the top of the mountain to beg the scholars to inscribe them. He wanted written on the lid of the casket: "Longevity enduring as the mountain, Happiness deep as the sea." On the other plank, designed for a tablet for his raft to commemorate the honours he had received, he wanted inscribed: "Home of the Honest Fellow." But the scholars would write only the first.

III

By the time these two officials regained the capital, most of the other inspectors had come back one by one. Only Yu was still away. After resting at home for a few days, they were invited by their colleagues of the Water Conservancy Bureau to a great banquet to celebrate their return. Contributions towards the banquet were divided into three categories, Happiness, Honour, and Longevity, and the lowest charge was fifty big cowrie shells.[1] That day saw a veritable stream of fine horses and carriages, and before dusk fell hosts and guests had all assembled. Torches were lit in the courtyard, the appetizing smell of the beef in the tripods carried to the sentries outside and made their mouths water. When wine had been poured three times, the officials began to describe the scenery of the flooded areas they had visited, the reed flowers white as snow, muddied water gleaming like gold, fat, succulent eels, slippery duckweed. . . . As the wine went to their heads, they produced the specimens of food they had collected, packed in neat wooden caskets on the cover of which were inscriptions in the style of Fu Hsi's trigrams and Tsang Chieh's[2] "sobbing ghost" characters. First everyone admired the calligraphy and, after disputing till they nearly came to blows, decided that the first place should be given to the inscription: "The state is prosperous, the people at peace." For not only was the calligraphy so

---

[1] Used as money in ancient China.

[2] According to legend, Tsang Chieh was an imperial chronicler who invented the Chinese written language.

ancient as to be almost undecipherable, with a rude antique flavour about it, but the sentiments were thoroughly
appropriate, worthy to be recorded by imperial historians.

After this evaluation of an art which was a Chinese
speciality, cultural problems were set aside while they
investigated the contents of the caskets. The delicate
shapes of the cakes aroused general admiration. But,
perhaps because too much wine had been drunk, a note of
discord crept in. One took a bite of pine-bark cake and
was loud in his praise of its fresh flavour, declaring that
the next day he would resign to live in retirement and
enjoy this pure happiness. Another, who had tried a
cypress-leaf bun, pronounced it coarse in texture and bitter
to the taste; it had hurt his tongue; and this sharing in
the sufferings of the common people showed that not only
had the sovereign a hard lot — it was far from easy to be
a minister. Others rushed forward to snatch the cakes
and buns away from them, because there was soon to be
a fund-raising exhibition at which these should be displayed — it would look bad if there were bites out of
them all.

Meanwhile a tumult had arisen outside. A crowd of
rough, beggarly-looking fellows with black faces and
ragged clothes had broken through the barriers and were
rushing the bureau. The sentries, with a great shout,
thrust their gleaming lances one across the other to block
the way.

"What's this? — Use your eyes!" shouted the tall, thin
hulk of a man with huge hands and feet who was leading
the way, after a second's stupefaction.

The guards strained their eyes in the fading light, then
stood respectfully to attention, presenting arms, to let
the band pass. They stopped only a woman in a dark
blue homespun gown with a child in her arms, who came
panting up after the others.

"Here! Don't you know me?" she demanded in surprise, wiping the perspiration from her forehead with one clenched fist.

"Of course we know you, Mrs. Yu!"

"Why don't you let me in, then?"

"These are difficult times, ma'am. This year, to rectify public morality and reform men's hearts, there is segregation of the sexes. Not a yamen nowadays will admit a woman. That applies not only here, not only to you. These are orders from above, we're not to blame."

After a moment's bewilderment, Mrs. Yu turned away raising her eyebrows and cried:

"May you be hacked into a thousand pieces! Whose funeral are you rushing to? You passed your own home without so much as looking inside, rushing along as if your parents were dead! You're an official, an official! What's the use of being an official? Remember how your old man was sent into exile and fell into the lake to change into a huge tortoise! May they hack you into a thousand pieces, you heartless wretch! . . ."

By now there was a fine commotion in the great hall of the bureau too. When the feasters saw this troop of rough fellows rush in, their first thought was of flight. But when no weapons were brandished, they took courage and looked again at the new arrivals who were coming closer. Though the man in front was black and gaunt, from his manner they recognized Yu. The others, it goes without saying, were his followers.

This shock sobered them up. With a rustling of robes they retreated from their seats. Yu walked straight to the feast and took the place of honour. Either because he was lacking in politeness or because he had gout, he did not sit cross-legged but with legs outstretched, his big feet pointing at the officials. He had no socks and

43

the soles of his feet were covered with calluses the size of chestnuts. His followers sat on either side of him.

"Did Your Honour get back to the capital today?" respectfully inquired one official bolder than the rest, edging forward on his knees.

"Sit a bit nearer, all of you!" cried Yu, ignoring this question. "How did your investigations go?"

Advancing on their knees, the officials exchanged uneasy glances. They sat themselves down by the ruins of the feast, looking at the bitten pine-bark cakes and the ox-bones gnawed clean. Yet for all their embarrassment, they dared not order the cooks to clear away.

"May it please Your Honour," said an official at last, "things are not too bad — our impression was most favourable. Pine bark and water-weeds are quite plentiful; as for drink, they have a great abundance. The common people, good simple souls, are used to the life. As Your Honour must know, their powers of endurance are famed throughout the world."

"Your humble servant has drafted a plan for raising funds," said another. "We propose to hold an Exhibition of Curious Food, also inviting Miss Nu-wei to give a mannequin display. Tickets will be sold, but to draw larger crowds it will be announced that no collection will be taken at the exhibition."

"Very good." Yu nodded.

"The most urgent matter, however," declared a third, "is to send a squadron of large rafts forthwith to fetch the scholars to the higher ground. At the same time an envoy should be sent to the Kingdom of the Marvellous Artisans to let them know that we respect culture and that their relief should be delivered here each month. We have quite a good report here from the scholars, which affirms that culture is the life blood of a nation and scholars the soul of culture. So long as culture exists, China will exist. All the rest is secondary. . . ."

"They consider the population of China too large," said the first official. "A reduction would be the best means of securing peace.[1] In any case, the people are simpletons whose pleasure and anger, pain and joy are by no means as subtle as the fancies of the wise. To know men and judge events, the first thing is to be subjective. Take the case of Shakespeare. . . ."

"Rubbish!" thought Yu. But he raised his voice to say: "My investigations have shown me that the old method of damming was quite wrong. In future we must use channels. What do you gentlemen think?"

Silence like that of the tomb! A deathly look stole over the faces of the officials; many of whom felt unwell — tomorrow they would have to ask for sick leave.

"That was Chih Yu's method!" objected a bold young official, speaking angrily to himself.

"In my humble opinion, Your Honour had better withdraw that decision!" An official with a white beard and hair, convinced that the fate of the empire hung from his lips, screwed up his courage to risk his life on a firm protest. "Damming was the method of your late respected father. 'He is a filial son who for three years does not change his father's way.'[2] It is not yet three years since your father went up to heaven."

Yu made not a sound.

---

[1] One of the arguments often put forward by the pseudo-scholars and officials of that time dealt with "reducing the population." For instance, Chen Yuan in "Idle Chat" in the *Modern Review*, Vol. 3, No. 73 (May 1, 1926) strongly advocated birth control on the fallacious grounds that "not only is there no need to increase our population; even cutting it down by half would do no harm." There was a great deal of such talk at the time.

[2] A quotation from *The Analects of Confucius*.

"And think how much trouble your late respected father went to!" said an official with a grey beard and hair, adopted son of Yu's maternal uncle. "He borrowed the *hsi-jang*[1] from the Heavenly Emperor to dam the flood; and although he incurred the divine displeasure, the level of the water did sink a little. I think we should continue using his methods."

Yu made not a sound.

"You should finish the task which your father failed to accomplish, Your Honour," said a fat official sarcastically. But though he imagined from Yu's silence that he was on the verge of being convinced, the sweat stood out on his face. "Restore the family name by the old family method. Your Honour probably has no idea what they are saying about your late respected father. . . ."

"In short, the merits of damming have been proved throughout the world," hastily interposed the old white-haired official to prevent a gaffe on the part of his fat colleague. "All other methods are 'modern' — that was the error into which Chih Yu fell."

Yu smiled faintly. "I know. Some people say my father has changed into a brown bear, others into a three-legged tortoise; yet others accuse me of being out for fame or profit. Let them talk. I want you to know that I have charted the mountains and lakes, asked the opinions of the people, seen the question in its true light and reached a decision. Come what may, we must use channels. My colleagues here are all of the same opinion."

He raised a hand to point from one side to the other. The officials with the white beard and hair, grey beard and hair, small white face, fat and sweaty, fat but not sweaty, looked in the direction indicated. They could see nothing but two rows of black, gaunt, beggarly-looking

---

[1] Some legendary earth which kept growing and never diminished.

figures which neither moved, spoke nor smiled, as if cast in iron.

IV

Time passed quickly after Yu left. Imperceptibly from day to day the capital took on a more prosperous look. First some of the wealthy started wearing pongee; then oranges and pomeloes came on sale in the big fruit-shops while new materials hung in the silk shops, and good soya-bean sauce, shark-fin soup and sea-slugs in vinegar appeared on the tables of the well-to-do. Later still men had bear-skin rugs and jackets lined with fox skin, while their wives took to wearing gold ear-rings and silver bracelets.

One had only to stand at one's gate to see fresh sights. One day a cartful of bamboo arrows would pass, the next a load of pine boards; sometimes grotesque rocks to make artificial mountains were carried past, or live fish to be sliced to make porridge. You could even see cartloads of tortoises one foot two inches long, their heads tucked into their shells, being taken in bamboo cages to the capital.

"Mummy! Look at the big tortoises!" the children would shout, running out to surround the carts.

"Get out of the way, you scamps! These treasures belong to the emperor. Do you want to lose your heads?"

As more precious objects were brought to the capital, there came further news of Yu. Under cottage eaves, in the shade of roadside trees, many tales were told of him. The most popular was the one about how he changed into a brown bear at night, how with his mouth and paws he dredged the nine rivers, how he summoned the heavenly troops and heavenly generals to catch Wu Chih Chi, the monster who had started the flood, and imprisoned him under Tortoise Mountain. There was no more talk of the feats of Emperor Shun; at most reference was made to the worthlessness of the crown prince Tan-chu.

As word had long since spread of Yu's return to the capital, every day a crowd would gather in front of the pass to watch for his cortège. But it never came. News of him, however, coming thick and fast, began to sound more and more authentic. And at last on a morning neither cloudy nor clear he entered the imperial city in Chichow through a milling crowd of thousands. He was preceded by no regal insignia, only by a great band of beggarly-looking followers. He came last, a hulk of a man with huge hands and feet, a swarthy face and brownish beard. Rather bow-legged, he was carrying in both hands a great dark stone pointed at one end — the *Hsuan Kuei*[1] bestowed on him by Emperor Shun. Calling out repeatedly: "Make way there, please!" he pressed through the crowd to the imperial palace.

At the palace gates, the acclamations and comments of the people sounded like the roar of the waves of the River Cheh.

Emperor Shun on his dragon throne was getting on in years, and now a faint alarm mingled with his fatigue. He made haste to rise politely at Yu's entry. After an exchange of greetings, the minister Kao Yao made a few polite remarks. Then the emperor said:

"Speak words of wisdom to me."

"What is there to say?" replied Yu bluntly. "My one thought has been to keep hard at it every day!"

"Keep hard at it — what does that mean?" inquired Kao Yao.

---

[1] *Kuei* is a piece of jade with a pointed top which the barons held in court ceremonies and sacrifices. *Hsuan* means black.

"When the Great Flood swept the land, encircling mountains and engulfing hills, the people were swallowed up in the water," said Yu. "I went by carriage on land, by boat on the water, by sledge through the mud, by sedan-chair through the mountains. On each mountain I felled trees, and with the help of Yi saw that everyone had rice and meat to eat. I let the water in the fields into the rivers, the water in the rivers into the sea; and with the help of Chi distributed sorely needed supplies to the people. Wherever there was a shortage, I made it good from districts with something to spare. And I moved the inhabitants. So at last everyone has settled down in peace everywhere and order reigns."

"Good! These are words of wisdom," approved Kao Yao.

"Ah!" said Yu, "to rule, one must be prudent and calm. Keep faith with Heaven, and Heaven will deal kindly with you as of old."

Emperor Shun, with a sigh, entrusted affairs of state to him, bidding Yu speak his mind freely to his face and not criticize him behind his back. When Yu had agreed to this, the emperor said with another sigh: "Don't disobey me like Tan-chu, who cares for nothing but dissipation, boats on dry land and makes such trouble at home that life is becoming impossible. He is quite insufferable!"

"I left home four days after my marriage," said Yu. "I have a son Ah Chi, but have never been a proper father to him. That is how I was able to curb the flood, divide the empire into five regions, each five thousand *li* square, with twelve provinces which extend to the sea. I have set up five governors, all good men except that of the Miao — you must keep an eye on him!"

"It is thanks entirely to your feats that my empire is in good shape again," approved the emperor.

Then Kao Yao and Emperor Shun, overcome by respect, together bowed their heads. And after the court was dismissed the emperor lost no time in issuing a special edict ordering everyone to follow the example of Yu or they would suffer the penalty.

That threw the merchants into a panic at first. But fortunately after his return to the capital Yu's attitude underwent a little change. Though he ate and drank simply at home, when it came to sacrifices or public occasions he made a great display. And though he dressed plainly in general, to go to court or return calls he put on splendid robes. So business was not affected, and before long the merchants were saying that Yu's ways were an excellent example to all, and Kao Yao's new laws were not bad. Then such peace reigned throughout the world that even wild beasts danced and phoenixes flew down to join in the fun.

November 1935

Gathering Vetch

I

For six months now, for no apparent reason, even the Old People's Home had lost its calm. Some of the old men indulged eagerly in whispered confabulations, running briskly in and out. Po-yi[1] alone held aloof from mundane affairs. It was autumn and chilly. Susceptible to the cold on account of his age, he used to spend the day sunning himself on the porch. Even hasty footsteps approaching could not make him look up.

"Elder brother!"

It was Shu-chi's voice. Po-yi, always a stickler for etiquette, stood up before raising his head, and with a gesture invited his brother to be seated.

"The political situation doesn't seem so good, elder brother." There was a quaver in Shu-chi's voice as he sat down breathlessly beside him.

"What is the matter?" Po-yi, turning, saw that his brother's pale face was even paler than usual.

"You must have heard about the two blind musicians who fled here from the king of Shang."

---

[1] Po-yi and Shu-chi were the sons of the king of Kuchu. Refusing to eat the grain of Chou they starved themselves to death in Shouyang Mountain when the Chou people conquered the Shangs.

"Yes, I believe San Yi-sheng mentioned them a few days ago. I paid very little attention."

"I called on them today. One is Grand Master Tzu, the other Junior Master Chiang. They have brought a number of musical instruments with them. Some time ago, apparently, they held an exhibition. All who saw it were loud in their praise — but it looks as if they're preparing here for a war."

"A war over musical instruments? That is not in accordance with the Kingly Way of old." Po-yi spoke with deliberation.

"Not simply over the music. You must know of the improper conduct of the king of Shang. When a man forded the river at dawn with no fear of the icy water, the king cut off his feet to examine the marrow of his bones. He tore out Prince Pi-kan's heart to see if it had seven orifices or not. All this was hearsay before, but since their arrival the blind musicians have confirmed it. They also bear out quite conclusively that the king of Shang has subverted the ancient laws. Whoever subverts the ancient laws should be attacked. To my mind, though, for a subject to attack his sovereign does not accord either with the Kingly Way of old. . . ."

"The pancakes have been getting smaller every day. That is a bad sign," said Po-yi after reflection. "But I advise you to go out less and to hold your tongue. Just keep up your shadow-boxing every morning."

"Yes. . . ." Shu-chi, an obedient younger brother, acquiesced quietly.

"Think for yourself." Po-yi knew he was not convinced. "We are guests here because the Earl of the West[1] respected old age. If the pancakes get smaller, it is not for us

---

[1] Chi Chang, King Wen of Chou, when he was still a vassal of Shang.

to complain — no, not even if something worse were to happen."

"Are we staying here, then, just to have a refuge in our old age?"

"Don't talk so much. I haven't the energy to listen."

Po-yi started coughing and Shu-chi said no more.

When the fit of coughing was over, complete silence fell again. The setting sun of late autumn made their white beards sparkle like snow.

II

The unrest increased from day to day, however. Not only did the pancakes become still smaller, the flour grew coarser too. In the Old People's Home there were more whispered confabulations. Outside they could hear the rumble of carriages and horses. Shu-chi was more eager than ever to go out and, though he said nothing on his return, his anxious expression made it hard for Po-yi to remain at ease. He had a presentiment that soon they would not be able to eat their bowl of rice in peace.

One morning towards the end of the eleventh month, Shu-chi rose early as usual for his physical exercise. Once in the courtyard he pricked up his ears, then opened the front gate and hurried out. He was back in about the time it takes to cook ten pancakes, panting and dismayed, his nose red with cold, his steaming breath coming in gasps.

"Get up, elder brother!" he shouted. "The war has started!" His voice was gruffer than usual as, hands respectfully at his side, he stood before Po-yi's bed.

Po-yi, who felt the cold, was most reluctant to get up so early. But being a kindly soul, at the sight of his brother's distress he gritted his teeth and sat up. He slipped his sheepskin-lined gown over his shoulders and slowly drew on his trousers under the quilt.

"I was just going to do my exercises," explained Shu-chi meanwhile, "when I heard the din of horses and men outside. I rushed straight out to the road and there they were! First came a big sedan-chair draped in white, with eighty-one bearers at the very least. In it was a wooden tablet with the words: 'Seat for the shade of King Wen of the great Chou Dynasty.' Behind was a troop of soldiers. I am sure they are marching against Shang. The present king of Chou is a filial son. When he starts a war he has King Wen's tablet carried before him. I didn't watch long, but when I came back I found a notice posted up right on our wall. . . ."

By now Po-yi was dressed and the brothers went out. The sudden cold made them cringe. To Po-yi, who seldom ventured forth, the scene outside the gate was full of novelty. A few paces and Shu-chi pointed to the wall where a large notice was posted:

OFFICIAL EDICT

Whereas Chou, king of Shang, obeying the wishes of his wife, has cut himself off from Heaven and neglected the three kinds of worship, alienating himself from his blood relations;

Whereas he has discarded the music of his ancestors and made licentious music, subverting the orthodox tunes to please his wife;

We hereby propose to inflict a just punishment on him, in accordance with the mandate of Heaven.

Go all out, men! Do not make it necessary for this edict to be issued twice or three times!

The two brothers remained silent after reading this, as they made for the main road. The roadsides were so thronged that not a drop of water could have trickled through. But when they asked to pass and the others turned and saw them, a way to the front was quickly made for these two white-bearded old men, in accordance with King Wen's order to respect the aged. The wooden tablet which headed the procession was already out of sight. Ranks of men in armour were passing. After the time it takes to cook three hundred and fifty-two large pancakes, there appeared more troops with nine-pointed flags over their shoulders like coloured clouds. After them, more men in armour. Then a great contingent of civil and military officials on fine big horses, escorting a prince with a brown face and whiskers who had a bronze axe in his left hand, a white ox-tail, used as a banner, in his right. He was a sight to impress all beholders! This was King Wu of Chou[1] going to "carry out the mandate of Heaven."

The people lining the road, overcome with awe, made not a movement, not a sound. In the utter silence, Shu-chi suddenly rushed forward pulling Po-yi with him. Dodging past several mounts, he seized the king's bridle and craned his neck to shout:

"Instead of burying your father who has just died, you make war — can this be called filial? As a subject you seek to kill your sovereign — can this be called virtuous?"

The crowd lining the road and the armed escort were at first frozen with horror. The ox-tail banner in the king of Chou's hand tilted. But after this speech by Shu-chi a great tumult broke out. Long swords were brandished over the brothers' heads.

"Wait!"

---

[1] Chi Fa, King Wen's son.

No one dared disobey an order from the Patriarch Chiang Shang.[1] Staying their hands, they stared at his plump round face — he too had a white beard and hair.

"These are just men — let them go!"

At once the officers lowered their swords and sheathed them. Four men in armour stepped forward, snapped to attention and saluted Po-yi and Shu-chi respectfully. Then, seizing the brothers, one man on each side, they marched them towards the pavement. The people promptly made way to let them pass.

When they reached the back of the crowd, the men in armour stood respectfully to attention again, let go of the old men's arms and gave each a hard shove in the back. With a cry, the brothers staggered forward for a few yards, then fell flat on the ground. Shu-chi, lucky enough to break his fall with his hands, simply had his face smeared with mud. Po-yi, who was older after all, knocked his head on a stone and fainted.

III

When the army had passed out of sight, the crowd turned to surround Po-yi and Shu-chi, the one prostrate, the other sitting on the ground. The few who knew them informed the rest that they were sons of the King of Kuchu in Liaohsi, who had ceded their right to the throne and taken refuge here in the Old People's Home founded by the last king. This announcement drew murmurs of admiration from the crowd. Some squatted down, their heads on one side, to peer at Shu-chi's face; others went home to brew a decoction of ginger; yet others went to inform the Old People's Home and ask for a door-flap to be sent at once to serve as a stretcher.

---

[1] Adviser to King Wu of Chou.

Enough time passed to cook a hundred and three or a hundred and four big pancakes. Since there were no fresh developments, the spectators drifted away. At last two old men hobbled up carrying a door-flap with straw spread on it — this was in conformity with King Wen's decree regarding respect to the aged. They set the door-flap down with such a clatter that Po-yi's eyes opened — there was life in him still! Shu-chi, with a cry of astonishment and joy, helped the old men lift his brother gently on to the improvised stretcher to carry him back. He walked alongside, his hand on the hemp cord holding the door-flap.

They had gone no more than sixty or seventy paces when they heard shouting in the distance:

"Hey! Wait a bit! Here's ginger!" A young matron was hurrying towards them with an earthenware pitcher in her hand. She was not running fast for fear, no doubt, of spilling the brew.

They stopped to wait for her and Shu-chi thanked her. Though she seemed a little put out to find that Po-yi had come round, she urged him to drink the ginger all the same to warm his stomach. But Po-yi, who had an aversion to anything hot, refused.

"What's to be done? This is ginger I've kept for eight years. Nobody else can give you anything so good. And no one in our family likes ginger. . . ." She was manifestly upset.

Shu-chi had to take the pitcher and prevail on Po-yi to sip a mouthful or two. There was still a good deal left, and pretending to have stomach-ache himself he drank it to the last drop. His eyelids turned red. But he complimented the woman on the potency of her ginger and thanked her once more. Thus he extricated Po-yi from this predicament.

After their return to the Old People's Home, they felt no undue ill effects. By the third day Po-yi was able to get up, though he still had a large bump on his forehead and no appetite.

Officials and private citizens alike refused to leave them alone. They were incessantly disturbed by government dispatches as well as by rumours. At the end of the twelfth month they heard that the army had forded the river at Meng, and that all the other feudal princes had rallied to them. Not long after, a copy of King Wu's *Great Declaration* was delivered. This had been specially written for the Old People's Home in characters the size of walnuts, out of consideration for their failing sight. Still Po-yi made no attempt to read it, contenting himself with listening to his brother's recital. In general he found nothing to object to, but his heart bled over certain phrases taken out of context, such as "abandoning his ancestors without performing the rites due to them, wickedly forsaking his country. . . ."

And the rumours increased. Some said that when the army of Chou reached Muyeh it engaged the men of Shang in a great battle till the plain was strewn with corpses and sticks floated like grass on rivers of blood. Others related that though the king of Shang had seven hundred thousand soldiers, his troops refused to give battle. After the arrival of the Chou army led by the Patriarch Chiang Shang, the soldiers turned tail, opening a way for King Wu.

Despite the discrepancy between these accounts, one thing was certain — a victory had been won. And the truth of this was later confirmed by the news that the treasures of the Stag Tower and the white rice of the Great Bridge[1] were being carried back. Wounded soldiers kept returning too, proving that there must have been heavy fighting. Virtually all the soldiers able to get about

---

[1] The Stag Tower and the Great Bridge were storehouses of King Chou of Shang, the former for the storing of jewels, the latter for grain.

would sit telling tales of the war in tea-houses, taverns and barber's shops or under the eaves and before the gates of private houses. There was always an eager crowd hanging on their lips. Since it was now spring and not too cold out of doors, these recitals sometimes went on late into the night.

Po-yi and Shu-chi both suffered from indigestion and could not finish their portion of pancake at each meal. Their sleeping habits remained unchanged in as much as they retired punctually at nightfall; but they suffered from insomnia. Po-yi would toss and turn in bed till Shu-chi was so distracted and grieved that he often got up again and dressed to stroll in the courtyard or go through his physical exercises.

One night of stars but no moon, the other old men were sleeping peacefully but there was still a buzz of talk at the gate. Shu-chi, who had never eavesdropped in his life, found himself stopping to listen.

"That confounded king of Shang! As soon as he was beaten he rushed to the Stag Tower." The speaker was doubtless a wounded soldier back from the front. "Devil take him! He made a great heap of all his treasures, sat down in the middle and set fire to the lot."

"You don't say! Too bad!" commented the porter.

"Don't worry! He was burned, but not his treasures. Our king entered the land of Shang at the head of all the princes. They were welcomed by the citizenry in the suburbs of the capital. Our king told his officers to call out: 'Peace be with you!' Then the men of Shang kowtowed. In the city they found written in large characters on every door the words 'A Submissive People.' Our king drove straight in his chariot to the Stag Tower. When he found the place where the king of Shang had taken his own life, he shot three arrows at him. . . ."

"Why? For fear he wasn't dead?" asked someone else.

"Who knows? At any rate he shot three arrows, thrust at the body with his sword and swung his bronze axe — whizz! He cut off the head and hung it from a great white banner."

Shu-chi shuddered.

"After that he went to find the king of Shang's two concubines. But they'd already hung themselves. Our king shot three more arrows, thrust at them with his sword and cut off their heads with a black axe to hang on a small white banner. So. . . ."

"Were those two concubines really pretty?" put in the porter.

"Who knows? The flag-pole was high and there was a crowd milling round it. My wound was troubling me, so I didn't go too close."

"They say the one called Ta-chi was a fox-fairy. All the rest of her had changed except her back paws, which she kept bandaged up. Is that true?"

"Who knows? I didn't see her feet. But a lot of the women in those parts do fix up their feet like pigs' trotters."

Shu-chi was a man of moral principles. When the conversation strayed from a king's head to women's feet he frowned and ran back, stopping his ears, to his room. Po-yi, still awake, asked softly:

"Have you been doing physical exercises?"

Instead of replying, Shu-chi walked slowly over to sit on the edge of his brother's bed. Bending forward, he told him what he had just overheard. Both were silent for some time. At last Shu-chi, with a troubled sigh, whispered:

"Imagine his breaking all the rules of King Wen like this! . . . He's lacking not only in filial piety but in humanity, mind you! . . . After this, we can hardly go on eating his rice."

"What shall we do, then?"

"I think we'd better leave. . . ."

After a brief consultation, they decided to leave the Old People's Home the next morning to eat no more pancakes of the House of Chou. Taking nothing with them, they would make their way together to Mount Hua to subsist for their last years on berries and leaves. Besides, "Heaven is impartial, but it often favours the good." They might find birthwort or truffles.[1]

This decision lifted a great load off their minds. Shu-chi undressed again and lay down, and before long heard Po-yi talking in his sleep. His heart was glad within him. He could almost smell the rare aroma of truffles. Inhaling this fragrance he fell into a deep sleep.

IV

The next morning the brothers woke earlier than usual. They washed and combed their hair. Taking nothing with them — indeed, there was nothing to take except the old sheepskin-lined gowns they had on, the staffs in their hands and some left-over pancake — they left the Old People's Home as if for a stroll. But the realization that they were departing for good caused faint stirrings of regret and made them turn back more than once for a last look.

There were not many people about yet. They passed only some women with eyes still swollen from sleep, who were drawing water at the well. The sun was high by the time they reached the suburbs, and the streets became more frequented. Most of the passers-by were carrying

_____

[1] Roots which were believed to be beneficial to the aged.

themselves proudly, heads high; but they made way, as was customary, for the old men. They were now coming into more wooded country. Some deciduous trees, whose names they did not know, were already breaking into leaf as if hung about with a grey-green mist through which they glimpsed the darker emerald of pine and cypress.

Drinking in this space, freedom and beauty, Po-yi and Shu-chi felt they had recaptured their youth. A spring came into their step, their hearts were glad.

The next afternoon they reached a crossroad and did not know which way to take. They made courteous inquiries of an old man who approached them.

"What a pity!" he said. "A little earlier, and you could have followed the troop of horses that went by just now. Take this road. There are more forks ahead where you'll have to ask again."

Shu-chi recalled that at noon they had been overtaken by some wounded soldiers driving a number of old, lean, lame or mangy horses, who had nearly trampled them to death. They asked the old man where these horses were being taken.

"Don't you know? Now that our king has 'carried out the mandate of Heaven' he has no further need for armies. So he's 'sending the horses to the southern slopes of Mount Hua' while we 'herd our cattle on Peach Orchard Plain.' Ah, now the whole world will be able to eat its rice in peace!"

This news was like cold water dashed over the brothers. They trembled, but did not change colour. Having thanked the old man, they proceeded in the direction indicated. This grazing of horses on the southern slope of Mount Hua had shattered their dream, filling them both with misgivings.

Though their hearts misgave them, they walked on in silence. By evening they were near a wooded loess hill on which could be seen a few mud cottages. They decided to seek shelter there for the night.

They were ten paces or so from the foot of the hill, when out of the wood slipped five sturdy fellows in white turbans, dressed in rags. The foremost wielded a sword, the others four sticks. Ranged at the foot of the hill to bar the way, bowing their heads respectfully they cried:

"How are you, venerable gentlemen?"

The brothers recoiled in terror. Po-yi was quaking. Shu-chi, always the more capable, advanced to ask the men their names and business.

"I am Chiung-chi the Younger, Chief of Mount Hua," said the man with the sword. "I have brought my men here to trouble you gentlemen for a little toll."

"We have no money, Chief," replied Shu-chi courteously. "We are from the Old People's Home."

"Ah!" cried Chiung-chi the Younger, promptly assuming an air of great deference. "In that case you must be 'the two grand old men of the empire.' We, too, revere the teachings of our late king and have the utmost respect for old age. Hence we must beg you to leave us some souvenir." When Shu-chi said nothing, he brandished his sword and went on more loudly: "If you insist on declining, we shall be forced to conduct a respectful search in accordance with the will of Heaven and cast deferential eyes upon your venerable nakedness."

Po-yi and Shu-chi promptly raised both hands. One of the men with sticks removed their gowns, padded jackets and shirts to make a thorough search.

"It's true — these two paupers have nothing." He turned, disappointed, to report to Chiung-chi the Younger.

Observing that Po-yi was trembling, Chiung-chi the Younger stepped forward to clap him courteously upon the shoulder.

"Don't be afraid, sir," he cried. "Shanghai types would have stripped you naked but we are too civilized to stoop to such behaviour. If you have no souvenirs for us, that's our bad luck. Now off with you, gentlemen!"

Struck dumb, without even waiting to clothe himself properly, Po-yi made off at a run, followed by Shu-chi. They kept their eyes on the ground. The five brigands stood back, hands respectfully at their sides, to let them pass.

"Must you really be going?" they inquired. "Won't you stop for tea?"

"No, thank you. Not this time . . ." replied Po-yi and Shu-chi as on they ran, nodding repeatedly.

V

The sending of horses to the southern slope of Mount Hua and the presence there of Chiung-chi the Younger, chief of the mountain, made these two just men afraid to enter that region. After further consultation, they headed north. Setting out at dawn and not stopping to rest till dusk, they begged their way to Shouyang Mountain.

This was just the place for them. Neither too high nor too extensive, the mountain had no great forests where might lurk tigers, wolves or bandits. It was an ideal retreat. At its foot, gazing round, they saw fresh foliage of a tender green, earth a rich gold, and wild grass starred with tiny red and white flowers. The mere sight was enough to gladden the eyes and heart. Rejoicing, tapping their way up the path with their sticks, they finally reached the overhanging boulder at the top which afforded shelter. There they sat down to wipe their perspiration and take breath.

The sun was sinking in the west. Twittering and cheeping, birds were flying back to nest in the woods. It was less quiet now than during their ascent, but the novelty of their surroundings delighted them. Before spreading out their sheepskin-lined gowns to sleep, Shu-chi took out two large balls of rice with which he and Po-yi satisfied their hunger. This was all that remained of the food they had begged on the way. For the brothers had agreed that they would be unable to carry out their resolve "not to eat the grain of Chou" until they had gained Shouyang Mountain. Accordingly, they finished the rice this evening. Starting from the next day, they would not compromise but abide by their principles.

They were aroused early by the crows. They went back to sleep, not waking again till nearly noon. Po-yi, his back and legs aching, could not get up. Shu-chi had to go out alone in search of food. After walking for some time he realized that the advantages of this mountain neither too high nor too extensive and free from tigers, wolves and brigands, entailed certain disadvantages as well. For from the village of Shouyang at its foot came old men and women to cut wood. And since children also clambered up there to play, not a single edible berry could be found — they must all have been picked.

His thoughts turned naturally to truffles. But though there were firs on the mountain, they were not old enough to have truffles at their roots. Even if they had, without a hoe he had no means of extracting them. His thoughts turned next to birthwort, but having seen nothing but its roots he had no idea what the leaves were like; and he could hardly pull up all the plants on the mountain to examine them. Even if birthwort had been growing under his eyes, he would not have recognized it. He grew angry, his cheeks burned. He scratched his head for a while in desperation.

Then an idea struck him which restored his calm. He walked up to a pine tree and filled his pocket with pine-needles. Next he went to the stream and found two stones with which to crush these and remove their green coats. Having washed them, he mixed them into a sort of paste. This he carried back on a slate into the cave.

As soon as Po-yi saw him, he inquired:

"Well, third brother, did you find anything? My belly has been rumbling for some hours."

"There's nothing, elder brother. Let's try this."

He propped the slate up on two stones, put the pine-needle paste on it and made a fire of dry twigs underneath. After a long, long time, the moist pine paste started to bubble, giving off an aroma which made their mouths water. Shu-chi smiled with satisfaction. He had learned this recipe at the banquet given on Patriarch Chiang Shang's eighty-fifth birthday, when he went to offer his congratulations.

Having given off an aroma, the paste rose, only to diminish in volume as it dried. It was a genuine cake. His hands in the sleeves of his sheepskin-lined gown, Shu-chi carried the slate with a smile to his elder brother. Po-yi blew on it, pulled at it and broke off a piece, which he stuffed into his mouth.

The longer he chewed, the more wrinkled grew his brows. He craned his neck and gulped several times, then spat out with an exclamation of disgust. Bending a reproachful look on Shu-chi, he told him:

"Bitter . . . coarse. . . ."

Shu-chi felt he had fallen into a deep abyss. All hope had gone. With trembling fingers he broke off a piece of the cake and started chewing it. No doubt about it, it was uneatable. Bitter . . . coarse. . . .

Losing heart, Shu-chi sat down hanging his head. He cudgelled his brains desperately, however, like a man struggling to clamber up out of an abyss. In fancy, he had become a child again, son of the king of Kuchu. He was on the lap of his nurse, a country woman who told him stories about the Yellow Emperor's victory over Chih Yu, Great Yu's capture of Wu Chih Chi, the famine which reduced the peasants to eating vetch.

He even remembered asking what vetch was like. And he had seen plants of this kind on the mountain! Strength came back to him. He stood up, strode into the undergrowth and set about his search.

Sure enough, there was no lack of vetch. In less than a *li* he half filled the skirt of his gown.

He washed the leaves at the bank and took them back, baking them on the slate on which he had cooked the pine needles. When the leaves turned dark green, he judged they must be done. This time he dared not offer them first to his brother. He helped himself to a pinch, and chewed it with closed eyes.

"What's it like?" demanded Po-yi anxiously.

"Delicious!"

Laughing, the two of them enjoyed the baked vetch. Po-yi, as elder brother, ate two extra pinches.

After this, they picked vetch every day. First Shu-chi did the picking alone, while Po-yi did the cooking. Then Po-yi felt strong enough to join in the search. Their recipes multiplied too: clear vetch soup, vetch broth, *purée* of vetch, boiled vetch, stewed vetch fronds, dried vetch leaves. . . .

By degrees, however, they finished all the vetch near by. And though they left the roots, fresh leaves were slow to grow. So every day they had to go further afield. They moved house several times, but the upshot was always the same. Gradually new lodging places became hard to find, for they wanted an abundance of vetch and proximity to water, and not many places on Shouyang

Mountain could offer both facilities. Shu-chi, fearful that Po-yi might get cold on account of his age, urged him to stay quietly at home to see to the cooking, leaving the picking of the vetch to him.

After some initial protests, Po-yi agreed, and this afforded him more leisure and comfort. But Shouyang Mountain was by no means deserted and as time went on, having nothing to do, his temper changed. Originally taciturn, he became talkative. He would chat with the children or with the wood-cutters. One day when perhaps he was in high spirits or someone had referred to him as an old beggar, he disclosed that he and his brother were sons of the King of Kuchu in Liaohsi — he was the elder son, his brother the third. His father had chosen the third son to succeed him, but at his death the third had insisted on deferring to him. Respecting his father's wishes, to save trouble he had fled. His third brother had done the same. They had met on the road and gone together in search of King Wen, Earl of the West, and entered his Old People's Home. However, since the present king of Chou had killed his sovereign, unable to eat the grain of Chou they had fled to Shouyang Mountain to live on herbs. . . .

When Shu-chi learned with dismay what Po-yi had disclosed, it was too late to stop him — the word had spread. Though he would not reproach his elder brother, he thought to himself: "Father showed foresight in not making him his successor."

Shu-chi's judgement proved correct: no good came of this. There was constant gossip about them in the village and men often climbed the mountain expressly to see them. They were regarded as great personages, as monsters, as rarities. They were followed to see how they gathered vetch, surrounded to see how they ate. All this with endless gestures and interminable questions, till their heads were fairly reeling. Yet they had to respond politely. For the slightest impatience, the least wrinkle of the brows would win them a reputation for "bad temper."

In general, public opinion was favourable. Later even some young ladies went to see them. But on their return these maidens shook their heads, declaring that the sight "wasn't worth the trip" — they had been grossly deceived.

At last they attracted the attention of Lord Hsiao-ping, foremost notable of Shouyang Village. This lord, the son-in-law of the adopted daughter of Ta-chi's maternal uncle, had the post of Master of Libations.[1] When he had seen that the mandate of Heaven was changing hands, he had gone with fifty carts of goods and eight hundred male and female slaves to declare his allegiance to the new king. Unfortunately this was merely a few days before troops massed at Meng Ford, and in the press of campaigning the king of Chou had no time to deal with him properly. He kept forty carts of goods and seven hundred and fifty of the slaves, giving him two hectares of fertile land at the foot of Shouyang Mountain and bidding him study the eight trigrams there. Lord Hsiao-ping also had a taste for letters; but all the villagers were illiterate, with no understanding of literary matters. Having nearly perished of boredom, he now ordered his servants to prepare his sedan-chair so that he might call on the two old men and talk with them of literature, especially of poetry. He was a poet himself, the author of a volume of verse.

But remounting his chair after their discussion, he shook his head. And on his return home he showed temper. To his mind, the two old fogeys were incapable of discussing poetry. Firstly they were poor. Searching all the time for

---

[1] In ancient times when there was a feast, some elderly men would offer libations with wine to pay homage to the gods, hence the name. From the Han and Wei Dynasties onwards, this became an official title, like libationer of the imperial academy, libationer of the imperial college, etc.

the wherewithal to support life, how could they write good poems? Secondly, being activated by "ulterior motives," they had no sense of the "moderation" of poetry. Thirdly, possessing pronounced views of their own, they had no sense of the "tolerance" of poetry.[1] Most deplorable of all, their characters were full of contradictions. Hence, carried away by righteous indignation, he declared categorically:

"Since 'all under the sky is our sovereign's territory,' isn't the vetch they eat our king's property too?"

Meanwhile Po-yi and Shu-chi were daily growing thinner. This was not due to social commitments, since their visitors were diminishing. The trouble was that the vetch was diminishing too and to gather a handful required a great expenditure of energy, a great deal of walking.

But troubles never come singly. When you fall into the well, a big stone nearby is sure to drop on your head.

One day they were eating their baked vetch, now so scarce that they were lunching in the late afternoon, when up came a woman in her twenties, unknown to them. She looked like the servant of a well-to-do family.

"Are you taking dinner?" she asked.

Shu-chi looked up and made haste to nod and smile.

"What is it?" she asked.

"Vetch," said Po-yi.

"What are you eating that for?"

"Because we don't eat the grain of Chou. . . ."

As Po-yi spoke, Shu-chi cast him a warning glance. But the woman, apparently very quick in the uptake, had caught his meaning at once. She gave a disdainful laugh. Carried away by righteous indignation, she declared categorically:

---

[1] In the *Book of Rites* Confucius was quoted as saying that moderation and tolerance were taught, and this became the criterion of literary composition and criticism in feudal China.

" 'All under the sky is our sovereign's territory.' Doesn't the vetch you're eating belong to our king too?"

Po-yi and Shu-chi heard every word distinctly. The conclusion, bursting upon them like a clap of thunder, made them both faint away. When they came to themselves, the woman had gone. They did not finish the vetch — they could not have swallowed it and the mere sight shamed them. But they could not raise their hands to sweep it aside. Their arms seemed to weigh hundreds of pounds.

VI

It was a wood-cutter who, about twenty days later, happened upon the bodies of Po-yi and Shu-chi, curled up in a cave behind the mountain. Their corpses had not decomposed, and while this was due in part to emaciation it also showed that they had not been long dead. Their old sheepskin gowns had disappeared, none knew where. News of this, reaching the village, caused quite a stir and a crowd of the curious streamed up and down the mountain till nightfall. Then a few busybodies covered the corpses with earth and discussed erecting a stone tablet with an inscription for the benefit of posterity.

Since none of the villagers could write, they asked Lord Hsiao-ping's assistance.

Lord Hsiao-ping refused to write an inscription.

"For that pair of fools? They don't deserve one. They went to the Old People's Home, all right! But they wouldn't steer clear of politics. They came to Shouyang Mountain, all right! But they would insist on writing poems. They wrote poems, all right! But they would express resentment, instead of knowing their place and

71

producing 'art for art's sake.' Tell me, does a poem like this have lasting value?

> We climb the Western Hill and pluck the vetch;
> A brigand replaces a brigand, not seeing his own fault.
> Emperors Shen Nung and Shun and the Hsia Dynasty have gone.
> Whom should we follow?
> Let us depart! Ours is an unhappy fate!

I ask you, what kind of rot is that? Poetry must be moderate and tolerant. Their scribblings are not merely 'lamentations' but downright 'abuse.' Thorns without flowers are not to be tolerated, much less out and out abuse. And leaving literature aside, to abandon the land of their fathers was not a filial act. To come here and censure government policy was not the conduct of good citizens . . . I refuse to write! . . ."

The illiterates could not follow all he said, but it was evident from his rage that he was against the scheme. They had to let the matter drop. This, then, was the end of the funeral preparations for Po-yi and Shu-chi.

But on summer nights, sitting outside in the cool, they sometimes talked of the two brothers. Some said they had died of old age, others of illness, yet others that they had been murdered by the brigands who stole their sheepskin gowns. Later on it was suggested that they had deliberately starved themselves to death, for Ah-chin, the maid servant in Lord Hsiao-ping's house, let it be known that a fortnight or so previously she had gone up the mountain to make fun of them. The simpletons, easily angry, must have stopped eating in a fit of temper. But all this had achieved was their own death.

This won Ah-chin many admirers, who paid tribute to her intelligence, though some reproached her with cruelty.

Ah-chin, for her part, did not hold herself in any way responsible for the death of Po-yi and Shu-chi. It was true, of course, that she had gone up the mountain to tease them; but that had simply been a joke. It was true, too, that the idiots had lost their temper and stopped eating vetch. But far from killing them, that had brought them unlooked for good fortune.

"Heaven is very kind," she said. "When he saw them sulking and nearly dying of hunger, he ordered a doe to suckle them. I ask you, what could be pleasanter than that? No need to till the soil, no need to cut wood; you sit there day after day while doe's milk flows into your mouth. But the old wretches didn't know when they were well off. That Number Three, whatever his name was, always wanted more. Doe's milk wasn't good enough for him. Drinking the milk, he thought: 'This doe is fat! If we killed her, how good she'd taste!' He reached slowly out for a stone. But that was a divine doe who knew men's thoughts. She made off like a streak of smoke. And the God of Heaven, disgusted by their greed, told the doe not to go any more. So you see they starved to death not because of anything I said but on account of their greed and hoggishness. . . ."

All her listeners heaved a deep sigh at the end of this recital. It seemed a great weight had been lifted from their shoulders. Whenever they recalled Po-yi and Shu-chi afterwards, they saw them as indistinct figures squatting at the foot of a cliff, opening wide their white-bearded mouths to devour the doe.

December 1935

Forging the Swords

I

Mei Chien Chih had no sooner lain down beside his mother than rats came out to gnaw the wooden lid of the pan. The sound got on his nerves. The soft hoots he gave had some effect at first, but presently the rats ignored him, crunching and munching as they pleased. He dared not make a loud noise to drive them away, for fear of waking his mother, so tired by her labours during the day that she had fallen asleep as soon as her head touched the pillow.

After a long time silence fell. He was dozing off when a sudden splash made him open his eyes with a start. He heard the rasping of claws against earthenware.

"Good! I hope you drown!" he thought gleefully and sat up quietly.

He got down from the bed and picked his way by the light of the moon to the door. He groped for the fire stick behind it, lit a chip of pine wood and lighted up the water vat. Sure enough, a huge rat had fallen in. There was too little water inside for it to get out. It was just swimming round, scrabbling at the side of the vat.

"Serves you right!" the boy exulted. This was one of the creatures that kept him awake every night by gnawing the furniture. He stuck the torch into a small hole in the mud wall to gloat over the sight, till the beady eyes revolted him and reaching for a dried reed he pushed the creature under the water. After a time he removed the reed and the rat, coming to the surface, went on swimming round and scrabbling at the side of the vat, but less powerfully than before. Its eyes were under water — all that could be seen was the red tip of a small pointed nose, snuffling desperately.

For some time he had had an aversion to red-nosed people. Yet now this small pointed red nose struck him as pathetic. He thrust his reed under the creature's belly. The rat clutched at it, and after catching its breath clambered up it. But the sight of its whole body — sopping black fur, bloated belly, worm-like tail — struck him again as so revolting that he hastily shook the reed. The rat dropped back with a splash into the vat. Then he hit it several times over the head to make it sink.

Now the pine chip had been changed six times. The rat, exhausted, was floating submerged in the middle of the vat, from time to time straining slightly towards the surface. Once more the boy was seized with pity. He broke the reed in two and, with considerable difficulty, fished the creature up and put it on the floor. To begin with, it didn't budge; then it took a breath; after a long time its feet twitched and it turned over, as if meaning to make off. This gave Mei Chien Chih a jolt. He raised his left foot instinctively and brought it heavily down. He heard a small cry. When he squatted down to look, there was blood on the rat's muzzle — it was probably dead.

He felt sorry again, as remorseful as if he had committed a crime. He squatted there, staring, unable to get up.

By this time his mother was awake.

"What are you doing, son?" she asked from the bed.

"A rat. . . ." He rose hastily and turned to her, answering briefly.

"I know it's a rat. But what are you doing? Killing it or saving it?"

He made no answer. The torch had burned out. He stood there silently in the darkness, accustoming his eyes to the pale light of the moon.

His mother sighed.

"After midnight you'll be sixteen, but you're still the same — so lukewarm. You never change. It looks as if your father will have no one to avenge him."

Seated in the grey moonlight, his mother seemed to be trembling from head to foot. The infinite grief in her low tones made him shiver. The next moment, though, hot blood raced through his veins.

"Avenge my father? Does he need avenging?" He stepped forward in amazement.

"He does. And the task falls to you. I have long wanted to tell you, but while you were small I said nothing. Now you're not a child any longer though you still act like one. I just don't know what to do. Can a boy like you carry through a real man's job?"

"I can. Tell me, mother. I'm going to change. . . ."

"Of course. I can only tell you. And you'll have to change. . . . Well, come over here."

He walked over. His mother was sitting upright in bed, her eyes flashing in the shadowy white moonlight.

"Listen!" she said gravely. "Your father was famed as a forger of swords, the best in all the land. I sold his tools to keep us from starving, so there's nothing left for you to see. But he was the best sword-maker in the

76

whole world. Twenty years ago, the king's concubine gave birth to a piece of iron which they said she conceived after embracing an iron pillar. It was pure, transparent iron. The king, realizing that this was a rare treasure, decided to have it made into a sword with which to defend his kingdom, kill his enemies and ensure his own safety. As ill luck would have it, your father was chosen for the task, and in both hands he brought the iron home. He tempered it day and night for three whole years, until he had forged two swords.

"What a fearful sight when he finally opened his furnace! A jet of white vapour billowed up into the sky, while the earth shook. The white vapour became a white cloud above this spot; by degrees it turned a deep scarlet and cast a peach-blossom tint over everything. In our pitch-black furnace lay two red-hot swords. As your father sprinkled them drop by drop with clear well water, the swords hissed and spat and little by little turned blue. So seven days and seven nights passed, till the swords disappeared from sight. But if you looked hard, they were still in the furnace, pure blue and transparent as two icicles.

"Great happiness flashed from your father's eyes. Picking up the swords, he stroked and fondled them. Then lines of sadness appeared on his forehead and at the corners of his mouth. He put the swords in two caskets.

" 'You've only to look at the portents of the last few days to realize that everybody must know the swords are forged,' he told me softly. 'Tomorrow I must go to present one to the king. But the day that I present it will be the last day of my life. I am afraid we shall never meet again.'

"Horrified, uncertain what he meant, I didn't know what to reply. All I could say was: 'But you've done such fine work.'

" 'Ah, you don't understand! The king is suspicious and cruel. Now I've forged two swords the like of which have never been seen, he is bound to kill me to prevent my forging swords for any of his rivals who might oppose or surpass him.'

"I shed tears.

" 'Don't grieve,' he said. 'There's no way out. Tears can't wash away fate. I've been prepared for this for some time.' His eyes seemed to dart lightning as he placed a sheath on my knee. 'This is the male sword,' he told me. 'Keep it. Tomorrow I shall take the female to the king. If I don't come back, you'll know I'm dead. Won't you be brought to bed in four or five months? Don't grieve, but bear our child and bring him up well. As soon as he's grown, give him this sword and tell him to cut off the king's head to avenge me!' "

"Did my father come back that day?" demanded the boy.

"He did not," she replied calmly. "I asked everywhere, but there was no news of him. Later someone told me that the first to stain with his blood the sword forged by your father was your father himself. For fear his ghost should haunt the palace, they buried his body at the front gate, his head in the park at the back."

Mei Chien Chih felt as if he were on fire and sparks were flashing from every hair of his head. He clenched his fists in the dark till the knuckles cracked.

His mother stood up and lifted aside the board at the head of the bed. Then she lit a torch, took a hoe from behind the door and handed it to her son with the order:

"Dig!"

Though the lad's heart was pounding, he dug calmly, stroke after stroke. He scooped out yellow earth to a depth of over five feet, when the colour changed to that of rotten wood.

"Look! Careful now!" cried his mother.

Lying flat beside the hole he had made, he reached down gingerly to shift the rotted wood till the tips of his fingers touched something as cold as ice. It was the pure, transparent sword. He made out where the hilt was, grasped it, and lifted it out.

The moon and stars outside the window and the pine torch inside the room abruptly lost their brightness. The world was filled with a blue, steely light. And in this steely light the sword appeared to melt away and vanish from sight. But when the lad looked hard he saw something over three feet long which didn't seem particularly sharp — in fact the blade was rounded like a leek.

"You must stop being soft now," said his mother. "Take this sword to avenge your father!"

"I've already stopped being soft. With this sword I'll avenge him!"

"I hope so. Put on a blue coat and strap the sword to your back. No one will see it if they are the same colour. I've got the coat ready here." His mother pointed at the shabby chest behind the bed. "You'll set out to-morrow. Don't worry about me."

Mei Chien Chih tried on the new coat and found that it fitted him perfectly. He wrapped it around the sword which he placed by his pillow, and lay down calmly again. He believed he had already stopped being soft. He determined to act as if nothing were on his mind, to fall straight asleep, to wake the next morning as usual, and then to set out confidently in search of his mortal foe.

However, he couldn't sleep. He tossed and turned, eager all the time to sit up. He heard his mother's long, soft, hopeless sighs. Then he heard the first crow of the cock and knew that a new day had dawned, that he was sixteen.

II

Mei Chien Chih, his eyelids swollen, left the house without a look behind. In the blue coat with the sword on his back, he strode swiftly towards the city. There was as yet no light in the east. The vapours of night still hid in the dew that clung to the tip of each fir leaf. But by the time he reached the far end of the forest, the dew drops were sparkling with lights which little by little took on the tints of dawn. Far ahead he could just see the outline of the dark grey, crenellated city walls.

Mingling with the vegetable vendors, he entered the city. The streets were already full of noise and bustle. Men were standing about idly in groups. Every now and then women put their heads out from their doors. Most of their eyelids were swollen from sleep too, their hair was uncombed and their faces were pale as they had had no time to put on rouge.

Mei Chien Chih sensed that some great event was about to take place, something eagerly yet patiently awaited by all these people.

As he advanced, a child darted past, almost knocking into the point of the sword on his back. He broke into a cold sweat. Turning north not far from the palace, he found a press of people craning their necks towards the road. The cries of women and children could be heard from the crowd. Afraid his invisible sword might hurt one of them, he dared not push his way forward; but new arrivals were pressing up from behind. He had to move out of their way, till all he could see was the backs of those in front and their craning necks.

All of a sudden, the people in front fell one by one to their knees. In the distance appeared two riders galloping forward side by side. They were followed by warriors carrying batons, spears, swords, bows and flags, who raised a cloud of yellow dust. After them came a large cart drawn by four horses, bearing musicians sounding gongs and drums and blowing strange wind instruments. Behind were carriages with courtiers in bright clothes, old men or short, plump fellows, their faces glistening with sweat. These were followed by outriders armed with swords, spears and halberds. Then the kneeling people prostrated themselves and Mei Chien Chih saw a great carriage with a yellow canopy drive up. In the middle of this was seated a fat man in bright clothes with a grizzled moustache and small head. He was wearing a sword like the one on the boy's back.

Mei Chien Chih gave an instinctive shudder, but at once he felt burning hot. Reaching out for the hilt of the sword on his back, he picked his way forward between the necks of the kneeling crowd.

But he had taken no more than five or six steps when someone tripped him up and he fell headlong on top of a young fellow with a wizened face. He was getting up nervously to see whether the point of his sword had done any damage, when he received two hard punches in the ribs. Without stopping to protest he looked at the road. But the carriage with the yellow canopy had passed. Even the mounted attendants behind it were already some distance away.

On both sides of the road everyone got up again. The young man with the wizened face had seized Mei Chien Chih by the collar and would not let go. He accused him of crushing his solar plexus, and ordered the boy to pay with his own life if he died before the age of eighty. Idlers crowded round to gape but said nothing, till a few taking the side of the wizened youth let fall some jokes and curses. Mei Chien Chih could neither laugh at such adversaries nor lose his temper. Annoying as they were, he could not get rid of them. This went on for about the time it takes to cook a pan of millet. He was afire with impatience. Still the onlookers, watching as avidly as ever, refused to disperse.

Then through the throng pushed a dark man, lean as an iron rake, with a black beard and black eyes. Without a word, he smiled coldly at Mei Chien Chih, then raised his hand to flick the jaw of the youngster with the wizened face and looked steadily into his eyes. For a moment the youth returned his stare, then let go of the boy's collar and made off. The dark man made off too, and the disappointed spectators drifted away. A few came up to ask Mei Chien Chih his age and address, and whether he had sisters at home. But he ignored them.

He walked south, reflecting that in the bustling city it would be easy to wound someone by accident. He had better wait outside the South Gate for the king's return, to avenge his father. That open, deserted space was the best place for his purpose. By now the whole city was discussing the king's trip to the mountain. What a retinue! What majesty! What an honour to have seen the king! They had prostrated themselves so low that they should be considered as examples to all the nation! They buzzed like a swarm of bees. Near the South Gate, however, it became quieter.

Having left the city, he sat down under a big mulberry tree to eat two rolls of steamed bread. As he ate, the thought of his mother brought a lump to his throat, but presently that passed. All around grew quieter and quieter, until he could hear his own breathing quite distinctly.

As dusk fell, he grew more and more uneasy. He strained his eyes ahead, but there was not a sign of the king. The villagers who had taken vegetables to the city to sell were one by one going home with empty baskets.

Long after all these had passed, the dark man came darting out from the city.

"Run, Mei Chien Chih! The king is after you!" His voice was like the hoot of an owl.

Mei Chien Chih trembled from head to foot. Spellbound, he followed the dark man, running as if he had wings. At last, stopping to catch breath, he realized they had reached the edge of the fir wood. Far behind were the silver rays of the rising moon; but in front all he could see were the dark man's eyes gleaming like will-o'-the-wisps.

"How did you know me? . . ." asked the lad in fearful amazement.

"I've always known you." The man laughed. "I know you carry the male sword on your back to avenge your father. And I know you will fail. Not only so, but today someone has informed against you. Your enemy went back to the palace by the East Gate and has issued an order for your arrest."

Mei Chien Chih began to despair.

"Oh, no wonder mother sighed," he muttered.

"But she knows only half. She doesn't know that I'm going to take vengeance for you."

"You? Are you willing to take vengeance for me, champion of justice?"

"Ah, don't insult me by giving me that title."

"Well, then, is it out of sympathy for widows and orphans?"

"Don't use words that have been sullied, child," he replied sternly. "Justice, sympathy and such terms, which once were clean, have now become capital for fiendish usurers. I have no place for these in my heart. I want only to avenge you!"

"Good. But how will you do it?"

"I want two things only from you." His voice sounded from beneath two burning eyes. "What two things? First your sword, then your head!"

Mei Chien Chih thought the request a strange one. But though he hesitated, he was not afraid. For a moment he was speechless.

"Don't be afraid that I want to trick you out of your life and your treasure," continued the implacable voice in the dark. "It's entirely up to you. If you trust me, I'll go; if not, I won't."

"But why are you going to take vengeance for me? Did you know my father?"

"I knew him from the start, just as I've always known you. But that's not the reason. You don't understand, my clever lad, how I excel at revenge. What's yours is mine, what concerns him concerns me too. I bear on my soul so many wounds inflicted by others as well as by myself, that now I hate myself."

The voice in the darkness was silent. Mei Chien Chih raised his hand to draw the blue sword from his back and with the same movement swung it forward from the nape of his neck. As his head fell on the green moss at his feet, he handed the sword to the dark man.

"Aha!" The man took the sword with one hand, with the other he picked up Mei Chien Chih's head by the hair. He kissed the warm dead lips twice and burst into cold, shrill laughter.

His laughter spread through the fir wood. At once, deep in the forest, flashed blazing eyes like the light of the will-o'-the-wisp which the next instant came so close that you could hear the snuffling of famished wolves. With one bite, Mei Chien Chih's blue coat was torn to shreds; the next disposed of his whole body, while the blood was instantaneously licked clean. The only sound was the soft crunching of bones.

The huge wolf at the head of the pack hurled itself at the dark man. But with one sweep of the blue sword, its head fell on the green moss at his feet. With one bite the other wolves tore its skin to shreds, then next disposed of its whole body, while the blood was instantaneously licked clean. The only sound was the soft crunching of bones.

The dark man picked up the blue coat from the ground to wrap up Mei Chien Chih's head. Having fastened this and the blue sword on his back, he turned on his heel and swung off through the darkness towards the capital.

The wolves stood stock-still, hunched up, tongues lolling, panting. They watched him with green eyes as he strode away.

He swung through the darkness towards the capital, singing in a shrill voice as he went:

Sing hey, sing ho!
The single one who loved the sword
Has taken death as his reward.
Those who go single are galore,
Who love the sword are alone no more!
Foe for foe, ha! Head for head!
Two men by their own hands are dead.

III

The king had taken no pleasure in his trip to the mountain, and the secret report of an assassin lying in wait on the road sent him back even more depressed. He was in a bad temper that night. He complained that not even the ninth concubine's hair was as black and glossy as the day before. Fortunately, perched kittenishly on the royal knee, she wriggled over seventy times till at last the wrinkles on the kingly brow were smoothed out.

But on rising after noon the next day the king was in a bad mood again. By the time lunch was over, he was furious.

"I'm bored!" he cried with a great yawn.

From the queen down to the court jester, all were thrown into a panic. The king had long since tired of his old ministers' sermons and the clowning of his plump dwarfs; recently he had even been finding insipid the marvellous tricks of rope-walkers, pole-climbers, jugglers, somersaulters, sword-swallowers and fire-spitters. He was given to bursts of rage, during which he would draw his sword to kill men on the slightest pretext.

Two eunuchs just back after playing truant from the palace, observing the gloom which reigned over the court, knew that dire trouble was impending again. One of them turned pale with fear. The other, however, quite confident, made his way unhurriedly to the king's presence to prostrate himself and announce:

"Your slave begs to inform you that he has just met a remarkable man with rare skill, who should be able to amuse Your Majesty."

"What?" The king was not one to waste words.

"He's a lean, dark fellow who looks like a beggar. He's dressed in blue, has a round blue bundle on his back and sings snatches of strange doggerel. When questioned, he says he can do a wonderful trick the like of which has never been seen, unique in the world and absolutely new. The sight will end all care and bring peace to the world. But when we asked for a demonstration, he wouldn't give one. He says he needs a golden dragon and a golden cauldron. . . ."

"A golden dragon?[1] That's me. A golden cauldron? I have one."

"That's just what your slave thought. . . ."

"Bring him in!"

---

[1] The ancient Chinese emperors, to bolster their prestige, often called themselves dragons. The dragon in Chinese legend was divine.

Before the king's voice had died away, four guards hurried out with the eunuch. From the queen down to the court jester, all beamed with delight, hoping this conjuror would end all care and bring peace to the world. And even if the show fell flat, there would be the lean, dark, beggarly-looking fellow to bear the brunt of the royal displeasure. If they could last till he was brought in, all would be well.

They did not have long to wait. Six men came hurrying towards the golden throne. The eunuch led the way, the four guards brought up the rear, and in the middle was a dark man. On nearer inspection they could see his blue coat, black beard, eyebrows and hair. He was so thin that his cheekbones stood out and his eyes were sunken. As he knelt respectfully to prostrate himself, on his back was visible a small round bundle, wrapped in blue cloth patterned in a dark red.

"Well!" shouted the king impatiently. The simplicity of this fellow's paraphernalia did not augur well for his tricks.

"Your subject's name is Yen-chih-ao-che, born in Wen-wen Village. I wasn't bred to any trade, but when I was grown I met a sage who taught me how to conjure with a boy's head. I can't do this alone, though. It must be in the presence of a golden dragon, and I must have a golden cauldron filled with clear water and heated with charcoal. Then when the boy's head is put in and the water boils, the head will rise and fall and dance all manner of figures. It will laugh and sing too in a marvellous voice. Whoever hears its song and sees its dance will know an end to care. When all men see it, the whole world will be at peace."

"Go ahead!" the king ordered loudly.

They did not have long to wait. A great golden cauldron, big enough to boil an ox, was set outside the court. It was filled with clear water, and charcoal was lit beneath it.

The dark man stood at one side. When the charcoal was red he put down his bundle and undid it. Then with both hands he held up a boy's head with fine eyebrows, large eyes, white teeth and red lips. A smile was on its face. Its tangled hair was like faint blue smoke. The dark man raised it high, turning round to display it to the whole assembly. He held it over the cauldron while he muttered something unintelligible, and finally dropped it with a splash into the water. Foam flew up at least five feet high. Then all was still.

For a long time nothing happened. The king lost patience, the queen, concubines, ministers and eunuchs began to feel alarmed, while the plump dwarfs started to sneer. These sneers made the king suspect that he was being made to look a fool. He turned to the guards to order them to have this oaf who dared deceive his monarch thrown into the great cauldron and boiled to death.

But that very instant he heard the water bubbling. The fire burning with all its might cast a ruddy glow over the dark man, turning him the dull red of molten iron. The king looked round. The dark man, stretching both hands towards the sky, stared into space and danced, singing in a shrill voice:

> Sing hey for love, for love heigh ho!
> Ah, love! Ah, blood! Who is not so?
> Men grope in dark, the king laughs loud,
> Ten thousand heads in death have bowed.
> I only use one single head,
> For one man's head let blood be shed!
> Blood — let it flow!
> Sing hey, sing ho!

As he sang, the water in the cauldron seethed up like a small cone-shaped mountain, flowing and eddying from tip to base. The head bobbed up and down with the water, skimming round and round, turning nimble somersaults as it went. They could just make out the smile of pleasure on its face. Then abruptly it gave this up to start swimming against the stream, circling, weaving to and fro, splashing water in all directions so that hot drops showered the court. One of the dwarfs gave a yelp and rubbed his nose. Scalded, he couldn't suppress a cry of pain.

The dark man stopped singing. The head remained motionless in the middle of the water, a grave expression on its face. After a few seconds, it began bobbing up and down slowly again. From bobbing it put on speed to swim up and down, not quickly but with infinite grace. Three times it circled the cauldron, ducking up and down. Then, its eyes wide, the jet-black pupils phenomenally bright, it sang:

> The sovereign's rule spreads far and wide,
> He conquers foes on every side.
> The world may end, but not his might,
> So here I come all gleaming bright.
> Bright gleams the sword — forget me not!
> A royal sight, but sad my lot.
> Sing hey, sing ho, a royal sight!
> Come back, where gleams the bright blue light.

The head stopped suddenly at the crest of the water. After several somersaults, it started plying up and down again, casting bewitching glances to right and to left as it sang once more:

> Heigh ho, for the love we know!
> I cut one head, one head, high ho!
> I use one single head, not more,
> The heads he uses are galore! . . .

By the last line of the song the head was submerged, and since it did not reappear the singing became indistinct.

As the song grew fainter, the seething water subsided little by little like an ebbing tide, until it was below the rim of the cauldron. From a distance nothing could be seen.

"Well?" demanded the king impatiently, tired of waiting.

"Your Majesty!" The dark man went down on one knee. "It's dancing the most miraculous Dance of Union at the bottom of the cauldron. You can't see this except from close by. I can't make it come up, because this Dance of Union has to be performed at the bottom of the cauldron."

The king stood up and strode down the steps to the cauldron. Regardless of the heat, he bent forward to watch. The water was smooth as a mirror. The head, lying there motionless, looked up and fixed its eyes on the king. When the king's glance fell on its face, it gave a charming smile. This smile made the king feel that they had met before. Who could this be? As he was wondering, the dark man drew the blue sword from his back and swept it forward like lightning from the nape of the king's neck. The king's head fell with a splash into the cauldron.

When enemies meet they know each other at a glance, particularly at close quarters. The moment the king's head touched the water, Mei Chien Chih's head came up to meet it and savagely bit its ear. The water in the cauldron boiled and bubbled as the two heads engaged upon a fight to the death. After about twenty encounters, the king was wounded in five places, Mei Chien Chih in seven. The crafty king contrived to slip behind his enemy, and in an unguarded moment Mei Chien Chih let himself be caught by the back of his neck, so that he could not turn round. The king fastened his teeth into him and would not let go, like a silkworm burrowing into a mulberry leaf. The boy's cries of pain could be heard outside the cauldron.

From the queen down to the court jester, all who had been petrified with fright before were galvanized into life by this sound. They felt as if the sun had been swallowed up in darkness. But even as they trembled, they knew a secret joy. They waited, round-eyed.

The dark man, rather taken aback, did not change colour. Effortlessly he raised his arm like a withered branch holding the invisible sword. He stretched forward as if to peer into the cauldron. Of a sudden his arm bent, the blue sword thrust down and his head fell into the cauldron with a plop, sending snow-white foam flying in all directions.

As soon as his head hit the water, it charged at the king's head and took the royal nose between its teeth, nearly biting it off. The king gave a cry of pain and Mei Chien Chih seized this chance to get away, whirling round to cling with a vice-like grip to his jaw. They pulled with all their might in opposite directions, so that the king could not keep his mouth shut. Then they fell on him savagely, like famished hens pecking at rice, till the king's head was mauled and savaged out of all recognition. To begin with he lashed about frantically in the cauldron; then he simply lay there groaning; and finally he fell silent, having breathed his last.

Presently the dark man and Mei Chien Chih stopped biting. They left the king's head and swam once round the edge of the cauldron to see whether their enemy was shamming or not. Assured that the king was indeed dead, they exchanged glances and smiled. Then, closing their eyes, their faces towards the sky, they sank to the bottom of the water.

IV

The smoke drifted away, the fire went out. Not a ripple remained on the water. The extraordinary silence brought high and low to their senses. Someone gave a cry, and at once they were all calling out together in horror. Someone walked over to the golden cauldron, and the others pressed after him. Those crowded at the back could only peer between the necks of those in front.

The heat still scorched their cheeks. The water, smooth as a mirror, was coated with oil which reflected a sea of faces: the queen, the concubines, guards, old ministers, dwarfs, eunuchs. . . .

"Heavens! Our king's head is still in there! Oh, horrors!" The sixth concubine suddenly burst into frantic sobbing.

From the queen down to the court jester, all were seized by consternation. They scattered in panic, at a loss, running round in circles. The wisest old councillor went forward alone and put out a hand to touch the side of the cauldron. He winced, snatched back his hand and put two fingers to his mouth to blow on them.

Finally regaining control, they gathered outside the palace to discuss how best to recover the king's head. They consulted for the time it would take to cook three pans of millet. Their conclusion was: collect wire scoops from the big kitchen and order the guards to retrieve the royal head.

Soon the implements were ready: wire scoops, strainers, golden plates and dusters were all placed by the cauldron. The guards rolled up their sleeves. Some with wire scoops, some with strainers, they respectfully set about bringing up the remains. The scoops clashed against each other and scraped the edge of the cauldron, while the water eddied in their wake. After some time, one of the guards, with a grave face, raised his scoop slowly and carefully in both hands. Drops of water like pearls were dripping from the utensil, in which could be seen a snow-white skull. As the others cried out with astonishment, he deposited the skull on one golden plate.

"Oh, dear! Our king!" The queen, concubines, ministers and even the eunuchs burst out sobbing. They soon stopped, however, when another guard fished out another skull identical with the first.

They watched dully with tear-filled eyes as the sweating guards went on with their salvaging. They retrieved a tangled mass of white hair and black hair, and several spoonfuls of some shorter hair no doubt from white and black moustaches. Then another skull. Then three hairpins.

They stopped only when nothing but clear soup was left in the cauldron, and divided what they had on to three golden plates: one of skulls, one of hair, one of hairpins.

"His Majesty had only one head. Which is his?" demanded the ninth concubine frantically.

"Quite so. . . ." The ministers looked at each other in dismay.

"If the skin and flesh hadn't boiled away, it would be easy to tell," said one kneeling dwarf.

They forced themselves to examine the skulls carefully, but the size and colour were about the same. They could not even distinguish which was the boy's. The queen said the king had a scar on his right temple as the result of a fall while still crown prince, and this might have left a trace on the skull. Sure enough, a dwarf discovered such a mark on one skull, and there was general rejoicing until another dwarf discovered a similar mark on the right temple of a slightly yellower skull.

"I know!" exclaimed the third concubine happily. "Our king had a very high nose."

The eunuchs hastened to examine the noses. To be sure, one of them was relatively high, though there wasn't much to choose between them; but unfortunately that particular skull had no mark on the right temple.

"Besides," said the ministers to the eunuchs, "could the back of His Majesty's skull have been so protuberant?"

"We never paid any attention to the back of His Majesty's skull. . . ."

The queen and the concubines searched their memories. Some said it had been protuberant, some flat. When they questioned the eunuch who had combed the royal hair, he would not commit himself to an answer.

That evening a council of princes and ministers was held to determine which head was the king's, but with no better result than during the day. In fact, even the hair and moustaches presented a problem. The white was of course the king's, but since he had been grizzled it was very hard to decide about the black. After half a night's discussion, they had just eliminated a few red hairs when the ninth concubine protested. She was sure she had seen a few brown hairs in the king's moustache; in which case how could they be sure there was not a single red one? They had to put them all together again and leave the case unsettled.

They had reached no solution by the early hours of the morning. They prolonged the discussion, yawning, till the cock crowed a second time, before fixing on a safe and satisfactory solution: All three heads should be placed in the golden coffin beside the king's body for interment.

The funeral took place a week later. The whole city was agog. Citizens of the capital and spectators from far away flocked to the royal funeral. As soon as it was light, the road was thronged with men and women. Sandwiched in between were tables bearing sacrificial offerings. Shortly before midday horsemen cantered out to clear the roads. Some time later came a procession of flags, batons, spears, bows, halberds and the like, followed by four cartloads of musicians. Then, rising and falling with the uneven ground, a yellow canopy drew near. It was possible to make out the hearse with the golden coffin in which lay three heads and one body.

The people knelt down, revealing rows of tables of offerings. Some loyal subjects gulped back tears of rage to think that the spirits of the two regicides were enjoying the sacrifice now together with the king. But there was nothing they could do about it.

Then followed the carriages of the queen and concubines. The crowd stared at them and they stared at the crowd, not stopping their wailing. After them came the ministers, eunuchs and dwarfs, all of whom had assumed a mournful air. But no one paid the least attention to them, and their ranks were squeezed out of all semblance of order.

October 1926

Leaving the Pass

Lao Tzu[1] was seated motionless, like a senseless block of wood.

"Master, Kung Chiu[2] is here again!" whispered his disciple Kengsang Chu, entering in some annoyance.

"Ask him in. . . ."

"How are you, master?" inquired Confucius, bowing respectfully.

"As always," replied Lao Tzu. "And you? Have you read all the books in our collection?"

"Yes. But. . . ." For the first time Confucius appeared a little flustered. "I have studied the Six Classics: *Book of Songs, Book of History, Book of Ritual, Book of Music, Book of Change*, and *Spring and Autumn Annals*. To my mind, after all this time, I have mastered them thoroughly. I have been to see seventy-two princes, none of whom would take my advice. It is certainly hard to make oneself understood. Or is it perhaps the Way that is hard to explain?"

"You are lucky not to have met an able ruler," replied Lao Tzu. "The Six Classics are the beaten track left by

---

[1] An early Chinese philosopher, founder of the "do nothing" school of thought. He was a citizen of the kingdom of Chu in the Spring and Autumn Period.

[2] Confucius.

the kings of old. How can they blaze a new trail? Your words are like a track which is trodden out by sandals — but sandals are not the same as a path." After a pause he proceeded: "White herons have only to gaze fixedly at each other, and the female conceives. With insects, the male calls from windward, the female responds from leeward, and she is impregnated. With hermaphrodites, one creature has a double sex and fecundates itself. Nature cannot be altered, destiny cannot be changed; time cannot be halted, the Way cannot be obstructed. If you have the Way, all things are possible; if you lose it, nothing is possible."

Like one clubbed over the head, Confucius sat there as if his spirit had departed, to all intents a senseless block of wood.

Eight minutes or so passed. He inhaled deeply and stood up to take his leave, having thanked the master as usual most courteously for his instructions.

Lao Tzu did not detain him. He stood up and, leaning on his stick, saw him to the library gate. Not till Confucius was about to mount his carriage did the old man murmur mechanically:

"Must you go? Won't you have some tea? . . ."

"Thank you."

Confucius mounted his carriage. Leaning against the horizontal bar, he raised his clasped hands respectfully in farewell. Jan Yu[1] cracked the whip in the air and cried: "Gee-up!" The carriage rolled off. When it had gone more than ten yards, Lao Tzu went back to his room.

"You seem in good spirits today, master." Kengsang Chu stood beside him, arms at his side, when Lao Tzu regained his seat. "You made quite a speech. . . ."

---

[1] A disciple of Confucius.

"Just so," rejoined Lao Tzu wearily with a faint sigh. "I said too much." A thought struck him. "Tell me, what happened to the wild goose that Kung Chiu gave me? Has it been dried and salted? If so, steam it and eat it. I have no teeth anyway, so it's no use to me."

Kengsang Chu went out. Lao Tzu, quiet once more, closed his eyes. All was still in the library but for the sound of a bamboo pole scraping against the eaves as Kengsang Chu took down the wild goose hanging there.

Three months went by. Lao Tzu was seated motionless, as before, like a senseless block of wood.

"Master! Kung Chiu is back again!" whispered his disciple Kengsang Chu, entering in some surprise. "He hasn't been here for so long, I wonder what this visit means...."

"Ask him in...." As usual, Lao Tzu said no more than this.

"How are you, master?" inquired Confucius, bowing respectfully.

"As always," replied Lao Tzu. "I have not seen you for a long time. No doubt you have been studying hard in your lodgings?"

"Not at all," disclaimed Confucius modestly. "I stayed indoors thinking. I begin to gain a glimmer of understanding. Crows and magpies peck each other; fish moisten one another with their saliva; the sphex changes into a different insect; when a younger brother is conceived, the elder cries. How can I, long removed from the cycle of transformations, succeed in transforming others? ..."

"Quite so," said Lao Tzu. "You have attained understanding."

No further word was said. They might have been two senseless blocks of wood.

Eight minutes or so passed. Confucius inhaled deeply and stood up to take his leave, having thanked the master as usual most courteously for his instructions.

Lao Tzu did not detain him. He stood up and, leaning on his stick, saw him to the library gate. Not till Confucius was about to mount his carriage did the old man murmur mechanically:

"Must you go? Won't you have some tea? . . ."

"Thank you!"

Confucius mounted his carriage. Leaning against the horizontal bar, he raised his clasped hands respectfully in farewell. Jan Yu cracked the whip in the air and cried: "Gee-up!" The carriage rolled off. When it had gone more than ten yards, Lao Tzu went back to his room.

"You seem in low spirits today, master." Kengsang Chu stood beside him, arms at his side, when Lao Tzu regained his seat. "You said very little. . . ."

"Just so," rejoined Lao Tzu wearily with a faint sigh. "But you don't understand. I believe I ought to leave."

"Why?" If a thunderbolt had struck from the blue Kengsang Chu could not have been more staggered.

"Kung Chiu understands my ideas. He knows I'm the only one able to see through him, and this must make him uneasy. If I don't go, it may be awkward. . . ."

"But doesn't he belong to the same Way? Why should you go?"

"No." Lao Tzu waved a dissenting hand. "Ours is not the same Way. We may wear the same sandals, but mine are for travelling the deserts,[1] his for going to the court."

"After all, you are his master!"

"Are you still so naive after all these years with me?" Lao Tzu chuckled. "How true it is that nature cannot be altered, destiny cannot be changed! You should know

---

[1] The deserts in northwestern China.

that Kung Chiu is not like you. He will never come back nor ever call me master again. He will refer to me as 'that old fellow,' and play tricks behind my back."

"I could never have thought it. But you are always right, master, in your judgement of men. . . ."

"No, at the beginning I also often made mistakes."

"Well then," continued Kengsang Chu after some thought, "we'll fight it out with him. . . ."

Lao Tzu chuckled again and opened his mouth wide.

"Look! How many teeth have I left?"

"None."

"What about my tongue?"

"That's still there."

"Do you understand?"

"Do you mean, master, that what is hard goes first while what is soft lasts on?"

"Precisely. I think you had better pack up your things and go home to your wife. But first groom my dark ox and sun the saddle and saddle-cloth. I shall want them first thing tomorrow."

On nearing Hanku Pass,[1] instead of taking the highway which led there directly, Lao Tzu reined in his ox and turned into a byway to make a slow circuit of the wall. He hoped to scale it. The wall was not too high, and by standing on the ox's back he could just have heaved himself over. But that would have meant leaving the ox inside. To get it across would have needed a crane, and neither Lu Pan[2] nor Mo Ti[3] was born at this time, while Lao Tzu

---

[1] A strategic pass through which the men of ancient times travelled to China's northwest.

[2] Also known as Kungshu Pan; skilful artisan and inventor of the state of Lu.

[3] The ancient Chinese philosopher Mo Ti, who founded the Mohist school. The work attributed to Mo Tzu which we have today was

himself was incapable of imagining such a contraption. In brief, hard as he racked his philosopher's brain, he could think of no way out.

Little did he know that when he turned into the byway he had been spotted by a scout, who promptly reported the fact to the warden of the pass. He had therefore gone a little more than twenty yards when a troop of horsemen came galloping after him. At the head rode the scout, after him the warden of the pass, Hsi, followed by four constables and two customs officers.

"Halt!" some of them shouted.

Lao Tzu hastily reined in his dark ox, motionless as a senseless block of wood.

"Well, well!" exclaimed the warden in surprise, having rushed forward and seen who it was. He leaped down from his saddle and bowed in greeting. "I was wondering who it could be. So it's Lao Tan,[1] the chief librarian. This *is* a surprise."

Lao Tzu made haste to clamber off his ox. He peered at the warden through narrowed eyes, saying uncertainly: "My memory is failing. . . ."

"Of course. Quite natural. You wouldn't remember me. I am Warden Hsi. I called on you some time ago, sir, when I went to the library to look up *The Essence of Taxation*. . . ."

Meanwhile the customs officers were rummaging through the saddle and saddle-cloth. One pierced a hole with his awl and poked a finger in to feel around. Then he strode off in silence with a look of disdain.

"Are you out for a ride round the wall?" asked Warden Hsi.

recorded by his disciples. This story is based on one of the chapters in that book.

[1] *I.e.,* Lao Tzu.

"No. I was thinking of going out for a change of air. . . ."

"Very good. Very good indeed. Nowadays all the talk is of hygiene. Hygiene is of paramount importance. But this is such a rare opportunity for us, we must beg you to stay in the customs house for a few days so that we may benefit by your instructions. . . ."

Before Lao Tzu could reply, the four constables pressed forward and lifted him on to the ox. One of the customs officers pricked the creature's rump with his awl, and the ox, drawing in its tail, made off at a run towards the pass.

Once there, they opened up the main hall to receive him. This was the central room of the gate-tower and from its windows nothing could be seen but the loess plateau outside, sloping down towards the horizon. The sky was blue, the air pure. This imposing fortress reared up from a steep slope, while to right and left of its gate the ground fell away so that the cart track through it seemed to run between two precipices. A single ball of mud would indeed have sufficed to block it.

They drank some boiled water and ate some unleavened bread. Then, after Lao Tzu had rested for a while, Warden Hsi invited him to give a lecture. Since refusal was out of the question, Lao Tzu assented readily. All was bustle and confusion as the audience took seats in the hall. In addition to the eight men who had brought him in were four more constables, two customs officers, five scouts, one copyist, one accountant and one cook. Some of them had brought brushes, knives and wooden tablets[1] to take notes.

Lao Tzu sat in the middle like a senseless block of wood. After a deep silence, he coughed a few times and his lips moved behind his white beard. At once all the others held their breath to listen intently while he slowly declaimed:

---

[1] Before the invention of paper records were made on bamboo or wooden strips, and any mistakes in the writing were scraped off with a knife.

The Way that can be told of is not an Unvarying Way;
The names that can be named are not unvarying names.
It was from the Nameless that Heaven and Earth sprang;
The named is but the mother that rears the ten thousand creatures, each after its kind[1]. . . .

The listeners looked at each other. No one took notes. Lao Tzu continued:

Truly, "Only he that rids himself forever of desire can see the Secret Essences";
He that has never rid himself of desire can see only the Outcomes.
These two things issued from the same mould, but nevertheless are different in name.
The "same mould" we can but call the Mystery,
Or rather the "Darker than any Mystery,"
The Doorway whence issued all Secret Essences.

Signs of distress were apparent on every face. Some seemed not to know where to put their hands and feet. One of the customs officers gave a huge yawn; the copyist fell asleep, letting slip his knives, brushes and wooden tablets with a crash on to the mat.

Lao Tzu did not appear to have noticed; yet he must have done so, for he went into greater detail. But since he had no teeth, his enunciation was not clear; his Shensi accent mixed with that of Hunan confused the sounds "l" and "n"; moreover he punctuated all his remarks with "Erh." They understood him no better than before. But now, as he went into greater detail, their distress became more acute.

To keep up appearances, they had to go through with it. But by degrees, some lay down, others sprawled sidewise,

---

[1] These and the following quotations are from *The Way and Its Power* translated by Arthur Waley.

as each occupied himself with his own thoughts. At last Lao Tzu concluded:

"The Sage's way is to act without striving."

Even when he fell silent, however, no one stirred. Lao Tzu waited for a moment, then added:

"Erh, that's all."

At this they seemed to wake from a lengthy dream. After sitting so long, their legs were too numb to get up immediately. But their hearts knew the same joy and astonishment as prisoners to whom an amnesty is declared.

Lao Tzu was ushered into a side-room and urged to rest. After drinking a few mouthfuls of boiled water he sat there motionless, to all intents a senseless block of wood.

Meanwhile, outside, a heated discussion took place. Before long four representatives came in to see him. The gist of their communication was: Since he had spoken too fast and failed to use the purest standard speech, no one had been able to take any notes. It would be a great pity if no record were left. Hence they begged him to issue some lecture notes.

"What was he talking about? I simply couldn't understand a word!" cried the accountant, whose own accent was a heterogeneous one.

"You'd better write it all out," said the copyist, using the Soochow dialect. "Once it's written out, you'll not have spoken for nothing."

Lao Tzu did not understand them too well either. But since the other two had put a brush, knife and wooden tablets down in front of him, he guessed that what they wanted was the text of his lecture. Since refusal was out of the question, he assented readily. As it was late, he promised to start the next morning. Satisfied with the result of these negotiations, the delegation left.

The next day dawned overcast. Lao Tzu felt out of sorts but he set to work, eager to leave the pass as soon as possible. And he could not do this without handing in his text. A glance at the pile of wooden tablets made him feel worse.

But without changing countenance, he sat down quietly and started writing. He cast his mind back to what he had said the previous day, and transcribed each sentence as he remembered it. That was before the invention of spectacles, and his dim old eyes, screwed up till they seemed mere slits, were under considerable strain. Stopping only to drink boiled water and eat some unleavened bread, he wrote for a whole day and a half, yet produced no more than five thousand big characters.

"That should do to get me out of the pass," he thought.

He took cord and threaded the tablets together, dividing them between two strings. Then, leaning on his stick, he went to the warden's office to deliver his manuscript and express his wish to leave immediately.

Warden Hsi was most delighted, most appreciative, most sorry to think of his leaving. After trying in vain to keep him a little longer, he assumed a mournful expression and gave his consent, ordering his constables to saddle the dark ox. With his own hands he took from his shelf a package of salt, a package of sesame and fifteen cakes of unleavened bread. These he put in a white sack previously confiscated, and presented to Lao Tzu for the road. He made it clear that this preferential treatment was reserved for senior authors. A younger man would have got ten cakes only.

With repeated thanks, Lao Tzu took the sack. He descended from the fortress, accompanied by all the others. At the pass, he led the ox by the bridle till Warden Hsi implored him to mount it; and after declining politely for some time, he let himself be persuaded. Having bid farewell, he turned the ox's head and it plodded slowly down the sloping highway.

Soon the ox was making rapidly off with big strides. The other watched from the pass. When Lao Tzu was seven or eight yards away they could still see his white hair and yellow gown, the dark ox and the white sack. Then dust rose covering both man and beast, turning everything grey. Presently they could see nothing but yellow dust — all else was lost to sight.

Back in the customs house, the others stretched themselves as if a load had been taken off their shoulders and smacked their lips as if they had made a profit. A number of them followed Warden Hsi into his office.

"Is this the manuscript?" asked the accountant, picking up one string of wooden tablets and turning them over. "It's neatly written at least. I dare say a purchaser for it in the market could be found."

The copyist stepped forward too and read from the first tablet:

" 'The Way that can be told of is not an Unvarying Way!' . . . Bah! The same old farrago. It's enough to make your head ache, I'm sick of the sound. . . ."

"The best cure for a headache is sleep," said the accountant, putting the tablet down.

"Aha! . . . I shall have to sleep it off. The fact is, I went expecting to hear about his love affairs. If I'd known we'd be in for all that mumbo-jumbo, I wouldn't have gone to sit there for hours in agony. . . ."

"That's your fault for misjudging your man." Warden Hsi laughed. "What love affairs could he have? He's never been in love."

"How do you know?" demanded the copyist, surprised.

"Didn't you hear him say, 'By inactivity everything can be activated'? That's your own fault again for going to sleep. The old man has 'ambitions high as the sky and a fate as thin as paper.'[1] When he wants everything to be 'activated,' he's reduced to 'inactivity.' If he started loving someone, he'd have to love everyone. So how could he fall in love? How dare he? Look at yourself: you've only to see a girl, pretty or ugly, to make eyes at her as if she were your wife. When you do get married, like our accountant here, you'll probably behave better."

Outside a wind sprang up. They felt rather chilly.

"But where is the old man going? What does he mean to do?" The copyist seized this chance to change the subject.

"According to him, he's going to the desert," said Warden Hsi caustically. "He'll never make it. He'll find no salt or flour out there — even water is scarce. When he starts feeling hungry, I've no doubt he'll come back."

"Then we'll make him write another book." The accountant brightened. "But he must go easy on the unleavened bread. We'll tell him the principle has been changed and we are encouraging young writers. We'll just give him five cakes of unleavened bread for two strings of tablets."

"He may not stand for that. He'll sulk or make a scene."

"How can he make a scene if he's hungry?"

"I'm just afraid no one will want to read such trash." The copyist made a gesture with one hand. "We may not even get back the cost of five cakes. For instance, if what he says is true, our chief should give up his job as warden of the pass. That's the only way to achieve inactivity and become someone really important. . . ."

"Don't worry," said the accountant. "Some people will read it. Aren't there plenty of retired wardens and plenty of hermits who haven't yet become wardens? . . ."

---

[1] A phrase from the famous classical Chinese novel *The Dream of the Red Chamber*.

Outside a wind sprang up, swirling yellow dust to darken half the sky. The warden glanced towards the door and saw several constables and scouts still standing there, listening to their conversation.

"What are you gaping at?" he shouted. "Dusk is falling. Isn't this the time when contraband goods are smuggled over the wall? Go and make your rounds!"

The men outside streaked off like smoke. The men inside fell silent. Both copyist and accountant withdrew. Warden Hsi dusted his desk with his sleeve, then picked up the two strings of tablets and put them on the shelves piled high with salt, sesame, cloth, beans, unleavened bread and other confiscated goods.

December 1935

Opposing Aggression

I

Kungsun Kao, Tzu Hsia's disciple,[1] had called on Mo Tzu[2] several times but always found him out. Not till the fourth or fifth visit did he manage to meet him, for Mo Tzu came back just as Kungsun Kao reached his gate. They went inside together.

After the preliminary courtesies, Kungsun Kao, his eyes on the holes in the mat, asked politely:

"You are against war, master?"

"I am," said Mo Tzu.

"You mean, superior men shouldn't fight?"

"They should not," said Mo Tzu.

"But if even pigs and dogs fight, surely men. . . ."

"Ah, you Confucians! You pay lip-service to Yao and Shun,[3] but in practice model yourselves on pigs and dogs. How pitiful!" Mo Tzu stood up and hurried to the kitchen, saying: "You don't understand me. . . ."

Having passed through the kitchen to the well by the back door, he turned the windlass, drew half a pitcher of

---

[1] Tzu Hsia was a disciple of Confucius. His pupil Kungsun Kao is probably fictitious.

[2] See note in the story "Leaving the Pass."

[3] Legendary sage emperors.

water and holding it in both hands swallowed more than ten mouthfuls. Then he put down the pitcher, wiped his mouth and, his glance falling on one corner of the garden, cried:

"Ah-lien! When did you get back?"

Ah-lien, who had seen him first, came running over to stand respectfully, arms by his side, while he greeted his master. Then, with some show of indignation, he said:

"I'm through! They don't practise what they preach. They promised to give me a thousand measures of millet, but only gave me five hundred. I couldn't stay."

"Would you have stayed if they'd given you more than a thousand?"

"Yes."

"In that case, you left not because they don't practise what they preach but because you were getting too little."

Mo Tzu ran back into the kitchen, calling:

"Keng Chu Tzu![1] Mix some corn-flour dough for me!"

Keng Chu Tzu, a spirited lad, had just emerged from the central room.

"Do you want provisions for more than ten days, master?" he asked.

"That's right," said Mo Tzu. "Has Kungsun Kao gone?"

"Yes," Keng Chu Tzu laughed. "He was in a proper temper. He says we love everyone indiscriminately, with no special respect for our fathers, just like wild beasts."

Mo Tzu smiled.

"Are you going to the kingdom of Chu, master?"

"Yes. So you've heard about it too."

While Keng Chu Tzu mixed the cornmeal with water, Mo Tzu took a flint and moxa punk to strike a light and kindled some dry chips to boil water. His eyes on the

---

[1] Keng Chu Tzu, as well as Tsao Kung Tzu, Kuan Chien-ao and Chin Hua-li, was Mo Tzu's pupil.

flames, he said slowly: "Our fellow countryman Kungshu Pan[1] keeps trying to use that knack he has to make trouble. It wasn't enough for him to invent grapnels and pikes[2] to make the king of Chu fight Yueh. Now he's thought up some sort of scaling ladder to induce the king to attack the state of Sung. How can a small country like Sung hold out against Chu? I must put a stop to this."

When Keng Chu Tzu had put the cornmeal loaves on to steam, Mo Tzu went back inside. He rummaged in the cupboard till he found a handful of dried salted wild spinach and an old copper knife. He also unearthed a tattered piece of cloth. When Keng Chu Tzu brought in the steamed loaves, Mo Tzu wrapped all these up together. Taking no change of clothes, not even a towel, he tightened his leather belt, walked down the steps, put on his straw sandals, shouldered his bundle and left without a look behind. His bundle was still emitting puffs of steam.

"When will you be back, master?" Keng Chu Tzu called after him.

"Not for twenty days or so," replied Mo Tzu, striding on his way.

II

By the time Mo Tzu crossed the frontiers of Sung, the strings of his straw sandals had broken three or four times and the soles of his feet were burning. When he stopped to investigate, he found that large holes had rubbed through the sandals so that his feet were callous and blistered. He continued on his way, quite regardless. As

---

[1] See note in the story "Leaving the Pass."
[2] Weapons used on warships in ancient China.

he walked he looked round: the country was by no means depopulated, but on all sides were signs of the ravages of years of flood and fighting — these were replaced less rapidly than the people. For three days he walked without seeing a single large building, a single sizable tree, a single animated human face, a single fertile field. And so he came to the capital.

The city wall was crumbling away, but here and there fresh masonry had been added. Beside the moat were heaps of mud, as if dredging had been going on. The only men in sight, however, were some loafers sitting by the moat, probably fishing.

"They must have heard the news," reflected Mo Tzu. He scrutinized the fishermen more closely, but none of his disciples were among them.

He decided to go through the town. Entering by the North Gate, he followed the main thoroughfare towards the south. The city, too, was bleak yet quiet. All the shops displayed notices of cuts in prices, but no customers were in evidence and not many goods. The streets were deep in fine yellow dust.

"And they want to attack a place like this!" he thought.

He observed nothing of particular interest the whole length of the main road, except poverty and weakness. News might have come of the imminent attack from Chu, but the citizens here were so used to being attacked that they considered it their fate and thought nothing of it. And since all were cold and hungry with nothing left except their lives, it did not occur to them to move away. The watchtower of the South Gate was already in sight when he saw a dozen or so men by the roadside listening to a speaker, perhaps a story-teller.

Drawing nearer, Mo Tzu noticed the speaker saw the air as he cried loudly:

"We'll show them the fine morale of the men of Sung! We're all ready to die!"[1]

Mo Tzu recognized the voice of his disciple Tsao Kung Tzu.

But instead of pressing forward to greet him, he hurried through the South Gate to continue on his way. After walking for another day and most of the night, he stopped to rest under the eaves of a cottage, where he slept till dawn. Then he went on again. His straw sandals, in shreds now, could not be worn any longer. Since there were still some loaves in his wrapper and he could not use that, he tore a strip off his robe to tie round his feet.

The cloth was so thin, however, that the rough country roads cut his feet and made walking even more difficult. That afternoon he sat in the shade of a small locust tree and undid his bundle to eat and rest his feet at the same time. In the distance appeared a burly figure trundling a heavy barrow towards him. The man set down the barrow when he was close and came up to Mo Tzu, calling, "Master!" He panted as he wiped the sweat from his face.

"Is that sand?" asked Mo Tzu, recognizing his disciple Kuan Chien-ao.

"Yes. To use against the scaling ladders."

"What other preparations have been made?"

"Some flax, ashes and scrap-iron have been collected; but it's uphill work. Those with property won't give, those willing to give have nothing. In most cases all we get is empty talk. . . ."

---

[1] The speech of Tsao Kung Tzu here parodies the Kuomintang government. After the Japanese imperialists occupied northeastern China, the Kuomintang government adopted a policy of capitulation, putting up no resistance but making empty speeches in an attempt to deceive the people. Tsao Kung Tzu represents spokesmen of the Kuomintang government.

"Yesterday in the city I heard Tsao Kung Tzu holding forth on 'morale' and 'death.' Go and tell him not to use such empty, mystical terms. Death is not a bad thing. It's not easy either. But we must die to benefit the people!"

"He's hard to speak to," replied Kuan Chien-ao, not too hopefully. "After two years here as an official, he's not too keen to talk to us."

"What about Chin Hua-li?"

"He's very busy. He's just been trying out his cross-bow. I expect he's studying the terrain outside the West Gate now. That would explain how he came to miss you. Are you going to Chu, master, to see Kungshu Pan?"

"I am. But there's no knowing whether he'll listen to me or not. So go ahead with your preparations. Don't count too much on my talking him out of it."

Kuan Chien-ao nodded and as Mo Tzu set off again he followed him with his eyes before trundling his creaking barrow back to the city.

III

Ying, the capital of Chu, was completely different from Sung. It had broad roads, neat houses and large shops well stocked with fine goods: snow-white linen, bright red paprika, dappled deerskins, plump lotus seeds. The passers-by, though shorter than the men of the north, wore spotless clothes and abounded in energy. Among them, Mo Tzu with his old jacket, torn gown and feet swathed in rags, looked like a regular beggar.

The big square packed with stalls in the centre of the city was crowded. This was the market and here four roads met. Mo Tzu asked the way to Kungshu Pan's house from an old man who looked something of a scholar.

Unfortunately, due to their different dialects, he could not make himself understood. He was just tracing the words on his palm when everyone burst into song — the celebrated singer Sai Hsiang Ling had launched into her *Hsia-li-pa-jen*,[1] whereupon men and women from all over the country had joined in as if with one voice. Soon even the old scholar was humming too. Realizing that the man would not come back to look at the words on his palm, Mo Tzu made off without finishing the character *kung*. But everywhere there was singing; he could not get a word in. Peace was not restored till some time later, when presumably the singer came to the end of her song. Then Mo Tzu found a carpenter's shop and asked there for Kungshu Pan's address.

"Mr. Kungshu from Shantung who made the grapnels and pikes?" The carpenter, a fat man with a yellow face and black moustache, was evidently well informed. "It's not far. Turn back past the crossroad and take the second lane on the right. Go east, then south, then north again, and the third house is his."

After tracing the name on his palm once more so that the carpenter could confirm that there was no mistake, Mo Tzu fixed the directions in his mind. Then he thanked the man and strode off towards the place indicated. Sure enough, over the gate of the third house was nailed a finely carved hard wood board inscribed with six words in the ancient script: Residence of Kungshu Pan of Lu.

Rap! Rap! Mo Tzu banged the red copper knocker in the form of a beast. He was surprised by the appearance of a porter with knitted brows and angry eyes, who shouted:

---

[1] A common name for the folk music of the state of Chu in ancient China.

"My master is not seeing anyone! Too many of your compatriots have come here asking for money!"

Mo Tzu had barely time to throw him a glance before the door slammed shut. He knocked again, but there was no sound inside. That one glance had made the porter uneasy, however, and he went in to report to his master. Kungshu Pan, a carpenter's square in his hand, was measuring his model of the scaling ladder.

"Master, another of your compatriots is asking to see you . . . " whispered the porter. "He's rather a strange-looking man. . . . "

"What's his name?"

"I haven't asked. . . ." The porter was visibly afraid.

"What does he look like?"

"Like a beggar. A man in his thirties. Tall, dark-complexioned. . . ."

"Ah! It must be Mo Ti!"

With a cry of astonishment, Kungshu Pan threw aside his model and carpenter's square to run down the steps. The porter, astonished in his turn, rushed ahead to open the gate. Mo Tzu and Kungshu Pan exchanged greetings in the courtyard.

"So it is you!" Kungshu Pan, extremely pleased, ushered him into the central room. "Have you kept well? Are you as busy as ever?"

"Yes, it's the same old story. . . ."

"But you've come all this way — you must have some instructions for me."

"A fellow in the north has insulted me," said Mo Tzu calmly. "I want you to go and kill him. . . ."

Kungshu Pan felt annoyed.

"I'll pay you ten dollars," continued Mo Tzu.

This was more than his host could stomach. His face lengthened and he announced coldly:

"My conscience will not let me kill."

"Excellent!" Mo Tzu straightened up, much moved, and bowed to him twice. Growing calm again, he went on: "Let me tell you something, then. Up in the north, I heard you are making a scaling ladder for an attack on Sung. What wrong has Sung done? Chu has more land than it needs; it is short of people. To kill what you lack to get what you have more than enough of is no sign of intelligence. To attack Sung, which has done no wrong, is no sign of humanity. To know this, but not intercede, is no sign of loyalty. To intercede, but fail to persuade the king, is no sign of strength. To refuse to kill one man on the score of conscience, but be willing to kill many, is no sign of logic. What do you think, sir? . . ."

"Why. . . ." Kungshu Pan thought it over. "You are quite right, master."

"In that case, can't you give up this project?"

"Impossible." Kungshu Pan spoke regretfully. "I've already told the king about it."

"In that case, take me to see the king."

"Very well. But it's still early. Let's have a meal first."

Mo Tzu would not hear of this, though. He was bending forward, eager to rise — he could never sit still for long. Knowing his stubbornness, Kungshu Pan agreed to take him at once. First he went to his room to fetch clothes and shoes, saying frankly:

"But please change your clothes, master. This is not like at home — everything has to be handsome here. It would be better to change. . . ."

"All right. All right," Mo Tzu answered equally frankly. "It's not that I like wearing rags. . . . I just have no time to change. . . ."

117

IV

Since Mo Ti's fame as a sage of the north was known to the king of Chu, Kungshu Pan's introduction procured him an audience at once without any difficulty.

In clothes that were too short, like a long-legged heron, Mo Tzu accompanied Kungshu Pan into one of the rooms of the palace. Having made his obeisance to the king of Chu, he calmly embarked on this speech:

"There is a man who scorns his own covered carriage but covets his neighbour's rickety cart, scorns his own brocade robes but covets his neighbour's short felt jacket, scorns his own rice and meat but covets his neighbour's mess of husks and chaff. What would you call such a man?"

"A kleptomaniac," replied the king candidly.

"Chu has five thousand square *li* of territory to Sung's five hundred," said Mo Tzu. "That is like a covered carriage compared with a rickety cart. Chu has the Yunmeng marshes, well stocked with rhinoceros, stags and deer; it has the Yangtse and Han Rivers with an abundance of fish, turtles and crocodiles. No other state is so well off, while Sung lacks even pheasants, rabbits and carp. That is like rice and meat compared with a mess of husks and chaff. Chu has great pines, catalpas, cedars and camphors, while Sung has no large trees at all. This is like a brocade robe compared with a short felt jacket. In my humble opinion, the attack on Sung planned by Your Majesty's officers is on a par with this."

"No doubt about it!" The king of Chu nodded his agreement. "But since Kungshu Pan is already making a scaling ladder for me, we shall have to go through with it."

"Yet you can't be sure of the victory," said Mo Tzu. "If you have some pieces of wood, we can make a trial."

The king of Chu, who loved all novelties, cheerfully ordered his ministers to have wood brought forthwith. Mo Tzu took off his leather belt and bent it into the form of a bow with the arched side facing Kungshu Pan, to represent a city. He divided the wood into two parts of more than a dozen chips each. One half he kept, the other he gave to Kungshu Pan. These were their engines of defence and attack.

The two of them joined battle with these chips of wood, just as in a game of chess. When one side attacked, the other side warded it off; when one side withdrew, the other side gave chase. The king of Chu and his ministers could not make head or tail of what was happening.

They saw nine advances and retreats like this, as nine times, presumably, defenders and attackers tried different tactics. Then Kungshu Pan threw in his hand. Thereupon Mo Tzu pulled the arch of the belt to face himself, signifying that it was his turn to attack. Once more they battled, advancing and retreating; but in the third round one of Mo Tzu's chips reached the other side of the belt.

Though the king of Chu and his ministers were utterly at sea, the disappointment on Kungshu Pan's face as he put down his chip made it clear to them that he had lost both times, on the offensive as well as on the defensive.

The king of Chu felt a twinge of disappointment too.

"I know how to beat you," said Kungshu Pan sulkily after a moment. "I won't tell you, though."

"And I know how you mean to beat me," rejoined Mo Tzu calmly. "I won't tell you, though."

"What are you talking about?" asked the king, astonished.

"Kungshu Pan is thinking of killing me," Mo Tzu turned to answer. "He thinks once I am dead Sung will have no defenders and can be taken. But my disciple Chin Hua-li and three hundred others who are armed with defensive weapons made by me are waiting in the capital of Sung for an invasion from Chu. Even if I am killed, the city will hold out."

"Fine tactics, certainly!" The king was impressed. "In that case, I shall not attack Sung."

V

After dissuading Chu from attacking Sung, Mo Tzu's intention was to go straight back to Lu; but first he had to accompany Kungshu Pan home to return the clothes he had borrowed. It was now the afternoon. Both host and guest were famished. Naturally Kungshu Pan insisted that Mo Tzu stay to lunch — or rather to dinner — and urged him to spend the night there.

"No, I must be off today," said Mo Tzu. "I'll come back next year and bring the king of Chu my book."

"Isn't it all about justice?" asked Kungshu Pan. "Wearing yourself out body and mind to help those in danger and distress is all very well for the lowborn — not for the great. Remember that he's a king, my dear countryman!"

"That doesn't follow. Silk, hemp, rice and millet are all produced by the lowborn, but all desired by the great. This is even truer, surely, of justice."

"That's a fact." Kungshu Pan was in high spirits. "Before you came I wanted to conquer Sung. Now that I've seen you, I wouldn't take it as a gift, if it runs counter to justice. . . ."

"Then I will make you a gift of Sung." Mo Tzu was in high spirits too. "If you are just in all your dealings, I'll give you the whole world."

While host and guest were chatting and laughing, lunch was served. There was fish, pork and wine. Mo Tzu abstained from wine and fish, simply eating a little pork. When Kungshu Pan, drinking alone, saw with considerable embarrassment that his guest was making small use of his knife and spoon, he pressed some paprika on him.

"Go on! Help yourself!" he urged frankly, indicating the paprika sauce and pancakes. "Taste this. It isn't bad. But the onions here aren't as succulent as ours at home."

After a few cups, his spirits soared still higher.

"For naval battles I've invented grapnels and pikes. Does your justice have its grapnels and pikes? . . ."

"The grapnels and pikes of my justice are better than yours," replied Mo Tzu emphatically. "I grapple with 'love,' I ward off with 'respect.' Those who don't grapple with love lose men's affection. Those who don't ward off with respect are vulgarized. To be unloved and vulgar in men's eyes means being cut off. But mutual love and respect result in mutual benefit. If you attack others with grapnels and ward them off with pikes, they will pay you back in your own coin. The use of grapnels and pikes means mutual destruction. That is why the grapnels and pikes of my justice are better than those of your naval battles."

"But, my dear countryman, by insisting on justice you've as good as smashed my rice bowl!" Kungshu Pan changed the subject after this rebuff — no doubt also because he was tipsy. He had no head for drinking.

"At least that's better than smashing all the rice bowls in Sung."

"But that means I shall be reduced to making toys. Hold on while I show you some little things I've turned out."

He jumped up and ran into the room at the rear to rummage in a chest. Presently he was back with a magpie made of wood and bamboo. This he handed to Mo Tzu, saying:

"When this is wound up, it'll fly for three whole days. It's very ingenious, eh?"

"Not more than the wheels a carpenter makes." After a casual glance, Mo Tzu put the magpie on the mat. "Wood three inches thick, trimmed by a carpenter, can carry a load weighing fifty piculs. All that benefits mankind is ingenious and good; all that doesn't is clumsy and bad."

"Oh, I'd forgotten." This second rebuff sobered Kungshu Pan. "I might have known you'd say that."

"So just stick to doing justice," said Mo Tzu frankly, looking him in the eyes. "Then not only will you be considered ingenious, but the whole world will be yours. Well, I've taken up too much of your time. See you next year!"

With this, he picked up his wrapper and took his leave. Kungshu Pan, who knew it was out of the question to keep him, had to let him go. Having seen Mo Tzu out of the gate, he came back to his room and, after a moment's reflection, stuffed the model of the scaling ladder and the magpie into the chest in the room at the rear.

Mo Tzu made the return journey more slowly. In the first place, he was tired; in the second, his feet hurt; in the third, he had no rations left and was half starved; in the fourth, with this business settled he was not in such a hurry. He was even more unfortunate this time, though. Just over the border of Sung he was searched twice, while near the capital he met a band of National Salvation Collectors[1] who "collected" his tattered wrapper. Outside the South Gate he ran into a storm, and when he tried to

---

[1] Referring to the behaviour of the Kuomintang government at that time. Instead of resisting the Japanese aggressors, the Kuomintang made "popular organizations" collect funds to deceive and further exploit the people.

shelter under the city gate two patrolmen armed with spears chased him away. He was soaked to the skin, with the result that he suffered for over ten days from a heavy cold.

August 1934

Resurrecting the Dead

> *A stretch of wild country dotted with mounds, none of them more than six or seven feet high. There are no trees. Wild grass grows everywhere, with a path trampled through it by men and horses. Not far from the path is a pool. Buildings can be seen in the distance.*
>
> *Enter Chuang Tzu.*[1] *He has a thin, dark face and a grizzled beard. He is wearing a Taoist cap and cloth gown and carries a whip.*

CHUANG TZU: I've had nothing to drink since leaving home. It's no joke, this thirst. Far better change into a butterfly! But there are no flowers here. . . . Ah, I see a pool. What luck! (*He runs to the pool, clears aside the duckweed on the surface and scoops up some water. He drinks about a dozen mouthfuls.*) That's better. I'll start off slowly again. (*As he walks he looks round.*) Hullo, a skull! How did this happen? (*He parts the grass with his whip and taps the skull.*) Did greed, cowardice and dis-

---

[1] Chuang Tzu or Chuang Chou was a citizen of Sung in the Warring States Period. He was an officer at Chiyuan and an early philosopher, an exponent of Taoism. The book *Chuang Tzu* in thirty-three chapters is attributed to him. The story here is taken from a fable in the chapter "Supreme Joy" in this work.

regard for the right reduce you to this? (*Rap, rap.*) Did the loss of power and subsequent decapitation reduce you to this? (*Rap, rap.*) Or were you so disgraced that you could not face your parents, wife and children? (*Rap, rap.*) Don't you know that suicide is the act of a coward? (*Rap, rap, rap.*) Or did the lack of food and clothing reduce you to this? (*Rap, rap.*) Did old age and death long overdue reduce you to this? (*Rap, rap.*) Or was it . . . ? Bah, what a fool I'm making of myself here! How can it answer? Fortunately it isn't far now to the kingdom of Chu: there's no need to hurry. I'll ask the God of Fate to restore this man's form and flesh so that I can have a chat with him before he goes home to his people. (*Putting down his whip he turns towards the east, slowly raises his hands towards the sky and shouts at the top of his voice*): With all my heart I salute you, great God of Fate! (*The sky darkens, a wind springs up. A band of ghosts appears — tousle-headed and bald, thin and fat, male and female, old and young.*)

GHOSTS: Chuang Chou! Imbecile of an insect! Your beard is grizzled, yet you are still so dense! In death there are neither seasons nor masters. Space is time. Not even an emperor is so completely at ease. Don't meddle with what doesn't concern you, but hurry to Chu and attend to your own affairs. . . .

CHUANG TZU: You ghosts are the imbeciles. Although dead, you are still so dense. Don't you realize that life is death, that death is life, that the slaves are the masters? I, who seek the source of life, am not going to be influenced by you.

GHOSTS: All right, we'll make a fool of you straight away.

CHUANG TZU: With the king of Chu's edict on my head, I am not afraid of your monkey tricks, you little devils! (*Again he raises his hands to the sky and cries at the top of his voice*): With all my heart I salute you, great God of Fate!

> Blue is the sky, yellow the earth,
> The universe is a wilderness of chaos;
> Sun and moon wax and wane,
> The constellations are ranked in their places.
> Chao, Chien, Sun, Li,
> Chou, Wu, Cheng, Wang,
> Feng, Chin, Chu, Wei,
> Chiang, Shen, Han, Yang.[1]

By urgent order of the Taoist Patriarch, come hither! Come!
(*The sky clears, a wind springs up. The God of Fate appears indistinctly on the east side. He has a dark, thin face and grizzled beard and is carrying a whip. The ghosts fade away.*)

FATE: Chuang Chou, what are you up to now that you summon me? After quenching your thirst can't you rest content with your lot?

CHUANG TZU: Passing here on my way to visit the king of Chu, I saw a skull which still has the semblance of a head. This poor man must have had parents, a wife and children; yet he died here — the pity of it! I beseech you, Great God, to restore his form and flesh and bring him back to life so that he can go home.

---

[1] The first four lines are from the primer *The Thousand Characters,* the last four from the primer *The Hundred Names.* This is not a real Taoist incantation.

FATE: Ha, ha! You are not being honest with me. Before your belly is filled you start meddling in matters that are none of your business. You are never completely in earnest or completely in fun either. I advise you to stop disturbing me and go your way. Remember that "Fate determines life and death" and that I do nothing lightly.

CHUANG TZU: You are wrong there, Great God. In fact, there are no such things as life and death. I once dreamed that I turned into a butterfly, a butterfly flitting to and fro; but upon waking I was Chuang Chou, a desperately busy Chuang Chou. Not to this day can I be sure whether it was Chuang Chou who dreamed he was a butterfly or a butterfly which dreamed it was Chuang Chou. In the same way, how can we tell whether this skull is alive now or not, and whether what is called a return to life is not actually death? I hope, Great God, you will oblige me just this once. Since men have to be accommodating, gods should not be too rigid.

FATE (*with a smile*): You are one of those who can talk but not act. You are a man, not a god. . . . Very well, I'll show you.
(*The God of Fate points his whip towards the undergrowth. That same instant he vanishes. A flame springs up in the place at which he pointed and a man leaps to his feet. He is a tall, ruddy-faced fellow of about thirty, a peasant by the look of him. He is stark naked. After rubbing his eyes and pulling himself together, he catches sight of Chuang Tzu.*)

THE MAN: Ah?

CHUANG TZU: Ah? (*He advances, smiling, to look closely at the other.*) What happened to you?

127

THE MAN: Oh, I fell asleep. What happened to you? (*He looks round and gives a cry.*) Hey! Where are my bundle and umbrella? (*His eyes fall on himself.*) Hey! Where are my clothes? (*He crouches down.*)

CHUANG TZU: Steady on! Keep cool! You've just come back to life. Your things must have rotted away or been picked up by someone.

THE MAN: What's that you say?

CHUANG TZU: Tell me: What's your name? Where are you from?

THE MAN: I'm Yang the Elder of Yang Family Village. My teacher gave me the name Pi-kung.

CHUANG TZU: What were you doing here?

THE MAN: I'm on my way to see my relatives. I didn't mean to fall asleep here. (*Anxiously.*) But my clothes? My bundle? My umbrella?

CHUANG TZU: Steady on! Keep cool! Tell me: What period do you belong to?

THE MAN (*puzzled*): Eh? What period? I don't understand. . . . Where are my clothes? . . .

CHUANG TZU: Really! You're too stupid to live. Can you think of nothing but your clothes, you egoist? Without clearing up your own identity, how can you talk about clothes? That's why I asked in what period you lived. Never mind, you don't understand. . . . (*He reflects.*) Well, tell me this: What events were there in your village when you lived there?

THE MAN: Events? Plenty. Yesterday Second Elder Sister-in-law had a row with Seventh Grandmother.

CHUANG TZU: I don't call that an event.

THE MAN: You don't? . . . Well, Yang Hsiao-san received posthumous honours for filial piety. . . .

CHUANG TZU: That's more of an event, certainly. . . .
Still, it would be hard to find out when it happened.
(*He reflects.*) Did nothing even more important occur
— nothing to stir the whole place up?

THE MAN: Stir the whole place up? . . . (*He thinks.*)
Oh, yes! Three or four months ago, when they wanted
children's souls to put under the foundation of the
Stag Tower,[1] the whole village started squawking like
frightened hens. No time was lost in making amulets
for all the children to wear. . . .

CHUANG TZU (*startled*): The Stag Tower? When did
you say?

THE MAN: They started building it three or four
months ago.

CHUANG TZU: So you died in the reign of King Chou?
Extraordinary! You've been dead for five hundred
years and more.

THE MAN (*rather angrily*): We have only just met, sir,
you've no call to make fun of me. I simply took a
nap, why talk about being dead for five hundred
years? I'm a respectable man visiting my relatives.
Hurry up and give me back my clothes, my bundle
and my umbrella. I've no time to waste on jokes.

CHUANG TZU: Steady on! Let me think. How did
you come to sleep?

THE MAN: How did I come to sleep? (*Reflecting.*) I'd
got this far this morning when — wham! — I felt a
whack on my head. Everything went black, and I
fell asleep.

CHUANG TZU: Did it hurt?

---

[1] The place where the tyrant of the Shang Dynasty killed himself.
See "Gathering Vetch."

THE MAN: Not that I remember.

CHUANG TZU: I see. . . . (*He thinks.*) Yes . . . I understand. In the reign of King Chou of the Shang Dynasty you must have been walking alone this way when a highwayman set on you from behind. After killing you, he robbed you. This is now the Chou Dynasty, more than five hundred years later. How can you expect to find your clothes? Understand?

THE MAN (*glaring at Chuang Tzu*): No, I don't understand! Stop fooling, and give me back my clothes, my bundle and my umbrella. I'm a respectable man on my way to see my relatives. I've no time for fooling about.

CHUANG TZU: How stupid can a man be! . . .

THE MAN: Who's stupid? My things have gone and I find you on the scene. If you didn't take them, who did? (*He stands up.*)

CHUANG TZU (*desperately*): Listen to me: You were a skull till I took pity on you and asked the God of Fate to bring you back to life. Think for yourself! After being dead all these centuries, what clothes could you have? I don't ask for gratitude, but sit down and tell me what it was like in King Chou's time. . . .

THE MAN: You're raving. That talk wouldn't fool a three-year-old, and I'm thirty-three! (*Approaching him.*) You . . . .

CHUANG TZU: I assure you, I have the power. You must have heard of Chuang Chou of Chiyuan?

THE MAN: Never. And suppose you do have the power, what good is it? What's the use of coming back to life without a stitch on? Can I face my relatives like this? And my bundle's gone. . . . (*On

the verge of tears, he seizes Chuang Tzu's sleeve.)
I don't believe a word you say. You're the only one
here: You must give me back my things. I'll drag
you to the village head!

CHUANG TZU: Steady on! My clothes are old and
thin — don't tug like that. Here's a word of advice:
drop this obsession with your clothes. Clothes aren't
indispensable. Sometimes it is right to wear clothes,
sometimes it isn't. Birds have feathers, beasts have
fur, while cucumbers and egg-plants are quite naked.
This is why we say: "This may be right, but the
reverse may not be wrong." You can't say it is
right never to wear clothes; on the other hand can
you say it is always right to wear them? . . .

THE MAN (*losing his tempe*r): Confound you! Hand
back my things or I'll do you in! (*He raises a clenched
fist and seizes Chuang Tzu.*)

CHUANG TZU (*desperately, warding him off*): Don't
you dare! If you don't let go, I'll ask the God of
Fate to kill you off again.

THE MAN (*stepping back with a snigger*): All right.
Either kill me off again or give me back my clothes,
my umbrella and my bundle. In that bundle are
fifty-two coins, a pound and a half of sugar and two
pounds of dried dates. . . .

CHUANG TZU (*sternly*): Sure you won't regret it?

THE MAN: What do you think?

CHUANG TZU (*decisively*): So be it then! Since you
are such a dolt, we'll turn you back into what you
were before. (*He turns towards the east, raises his
hands to the sky and cries at the top of his voice*):
With all my heart I salute you, great God of Fate!

Blue is the sky, yellow the earth,
The universe is a wilderness of chaos;
Sun and moon wax and wane,
The constellations are ranked in their places.
Chao, Chien, Sun, Li,
Chou, Wu, Cheng, Wang,
Feng, Chin, Chu, Wei,
Chiang, Shen, Han, Yang.

By urgent order of the Taoist Patriarch, come hither! Come!
(*There is a long silence. Nothing happens.*)

Blue is the sky, yellow the earth!

By order of the Taoist Patriarch, come hither! Come! . . .
(*There is a long silence. Nothing happens.*)
(*Chuang Tzu looks around and slowly lowers his hands.*)

THE MAN: Am I dead or not?

CHUANG TZU (*disconcerted*): I can't understand why it didn't work this time. . . .

THE MAN (*rushing forward*): Enough of this nonsense! Give me back my clothes!

CHUANG TZU (*recoiling*): Don't you dare lay hands on me, you savage! What do you know about philosophy?

THE MAN (*grabbing him*): Thief! Brigand! I'll tear off your Taoist robe and take your horse to make up. . . .
(*Warding him off, Chuang Tzu pulls a whistle from his sleeve and blows three blasts. The man pauses in astonishment. The next moment a constable hurries in.*)

CONSTABLE (*shouting as he runs*): Stop him! Don't let him go! . . . (*When he approaches, we see he is a tall, sturdily built fellow from the land of Lu in regulation uniform and cap, holding a police baton. He has a red, beardless face.*) Stop him, the bastard! . . .

THE MAN (*seizing Chuang Tzu again*): Stop him, the bastard! (*The constable hurries up and grabs Chuang Tzu by the collar, brandishing his baton. The man lets go and bends forward to hide his nakedness.*)

CHUANG TZU (*catching at the baton and tilting his head*): What's the meaning of this?

CONSTABLE: The meaning of this? As if you didn't know!

CHUANG TZU (*indignantly*): I'm the one who called you — why have you arrested me?

CONSTABLE: What?

CHUANG TZU: I'm the one who blew the whistle. . . .

CONSTABLE: You mean you stole his clothes and then blew a whistle, you fool?

CHUANG TZU: I was passing this way when I saw him dead here and saved him. But he grabbed me and accused me of taking his things. Do I look like a thief?

CONSTABLE (*lowering the baton*): That's hard to say. "We know men's faces, not their hearts." Come along to the police station.

CHUANG TZU: Certainly not. I'm going to see the king of Chu — I must be on my way.

CONSTABLE (*letting go with a start and looking carefully at Chuang Tzu's face*): What, are you Chuang . . . ?

133

CHUANG TZU (*pleased*): Yes, I'm Chuang Chou of Chiyuan. How did you know?

CONSTABLE: Our superintendent has been talking a lot about you recently, sir. He said you were going to Chu to make your fortune, and might pass this way. Our superintendent is a recluse too, just holding this post on the side. He is one of your fans. He's read *On the Equality of Things*. For instance, "When there is life, then there is death; when there is death, then there is life. When there is possibility, there is impossibility; and when there is impossibility, there is possibility." What powerful writing! That's first class stuff, quite superb! Won't you come and have a short rest in our office?
(*The man backs away in dismay into the undergrowth and crouches down.*)

CHUANG TZU: It's late and I must be going. I can't spare the time. I shall call on your respected superintendent on my way back.
(*Chuang Tzu walks off as he says this and mounts his horse. Before he can crack his whip, the man leaps out of the undergrowth and rushes over to seize the bridle. The constable runs after him and catches his arm.*)

CHUANG TZU: Why are you still pestering me?

THE MAN: You're going off, leaving me with nothing. What shall I do? (*To the constable.*) Look, sergeant. . . .

CONSTABLE (*scratching the back of his ear*): It is difficult, I grant you. . . . Why, sir . . . it seems to me. . . . (*He examines Chuang Tzu.*) Since you're the better equipped of the two, why not give him a garment to cover his nakedness? . . .

CHUANG TZU: I would be glad to, as these clothes aren't mine by nature; but I'm on my way to see the king of Chu. I can't appear before him without my gown. And I can't take off my shirt and wear just a gown. . . .

CONSTABLE: True. You can't do without either. (*To the man.*) Let go!

THE MAN: I'm going to visit my relatives. . . .

CONSTABLE: Shut up! Any more trouble from you, and I'll take you to the police station. (*He brandishes his baton.*) Clear off!
(*The man retreats. The constable follows him into the grass.*)

CHUANG TZU: Goodbye, goodbye!

CONSTABLE: Goodbye, sir! Have a good journey!
(*With a flourish of his whip, Chuang Tzu rides off. The constable, his hands behind his back, watches him till he disappears in a cloud of dust in the distance. Then he slowly turns and starts back the way he came.*)
(*The man leaps out of the undergrowth and catches hold of his jacket.*)

CONSTABLE: What's the idea!

THE MAN: What am I to do?

CONSTABLE: How should I know?

THE MAN: I want to visit my relatives. . . .

CONSTABLE: Go ahead and visit them.

THE MAN: I've no clothes.

CONSTABLE: Must you have clothes to visit your relatives?

THE MAN: You let him go, now you want to clear off yourself. But I hold you responsible. Who else can I turn to? I can't go on living like this!

CONSTABLE: I warn you, suicide is the act of a coward.

THE MAN: Find me some way out, then!

CONSTABLE (*pulling away*): There's nothing I can do.

THE MAN (*seizing his sleeve*): Then take me to the police station.

CONSTABLE (*freeing his sleeve*): Impossible. I can't parade you stark naked down the street. Let go!

THE MAN: Lend me some trousers, then.

CONSTABLE: This is the only pair I have. If I lend them to you, I shan't be decent myself. (*He tugs himself free.*) Stop making trouble. Let go!

THE MAN (*catching him by the neck*): I insist on going with you!

CONSTABLE (*desperately*): Impossible!

THE MAN: You shan't leave here then!

CONSTABLE: What are you going to do?

THE MAN: I want you to take me to the police station!

CONSTABLE: Confound it! What use is that? Stop making trouble. Let go, or else. . . . (*He struggles with all his might.*)

THE MAN (*gripping him tighter*): Or else I can't face my relatives. I shall be less than human. Two pounds of dried dates, a pound and a half of sugar. . . . You let him go, I'll settle my scores with you. . . .

CONSTABLE (*struggling*): Stop that! Let go! Or else . . . or else. . . . (*He takes out his whistle and blows it wildly.*)

December 1935

故 事 新 编

鲁 迅 著

杨宪益、戴乃迭译

外文出版社出版（北京）

1961年（34开）第一版

1972年第二版

编号：（英）10050—484

00080

10—E—456P